Dear Reader,

What could be more romantic than a wedding? Picture the bride in an exquisite gown, with flowers cascading from the glorious bouquet in her hand. Imagine the handsome groom in a finely tailored tuxedo, his eyes sparkling with happiness and love. Hear them promise "to have and to hold" each other forever. . . . This is the perfect ending to a courtship, the blessed ritual we cherish in our hearts. And now, in honor of the tradition of June brides, we present a month's line-up of six LOVESWEPTs with beautiful brides and gorgeous grooms on the covers.

Don't miss any of our brides and grooms this month:

#552 HER VERY OWN BUTLER
     by Helen Mittermeyer
#553 ALL THE WAY by Gail Douglas
#554 WHERE THERE'S A WILL . . .
     by Victoria Leigh
#555 DESERT ROSE by Laura Taylor
#556 RASCAL by Charlotte Hughes
#557 ONLY YOU by Bonnie Pega

There's no better way to celebrate the joy of weddings than with all six LOVESWEPTs, each one a fabulous love story written by only the best in the genre!

With best wishes,

Nita Taublib

Nita Taublib
Associate Publisher/LOVESWEPT

WHAT ARE *LOVESWEPT* ROMANCES?

They are stories of true romance and touching emotion. We believe those two very important ingredients are constants in our highly sensual and very believable stories in the *LOVESWEPT* line. Our goal is to give you, the reader, stories of consistently high quality that may sometimes make you laugh, sometimes make you cry, but are always fresh and creative and contain many delightful surprises within their pages.

Most romance fans read an enormous number of books. Those they truly love, they keep. Others may be traded with friends and soon forgotten. We hope that each *LOVESWEPT* romance will be a treasure—a "keeper." We will always try to publish

LOVE STORIES YOU'LL NEVER FORGET
BY AUTHORS YOU'LL ALWAYS REMEMBER

The Editors

Charlotte Hughes
Rascal

BANTAM BOOKS
NEW YORK · TORONTO · LONDON · SYDNEY · AUCKLAND

RASCAL

A Bantam Book / July 1992

If you would be interested in receiving protective vinyl
covers for your Loveswept books, please write to this address
for information:

Loveswept
Bantam Books
P.O. Box 985
Hicksville, NY 11802

ISBN 0-553-44237-6

Published simultaneously in the United States and Canada

Bantam Books are published by Bantam Books, a division of
Bantam Doubleday Dell Publishing Group, Inc. Its trademark,
consisting of the words "Bantam Books" and the portrayal of
a rooster, is Registered in U.S. Patent and Trademark Office
and in other countries. Marca Registrada. Bantam Books, 666
Fifth Avenue, New York, New York 10103.

PRINTED IN THE UNITED STATES OF AMERICA

OPM   0 9 8 7 6 5 4 3 2 1

To my dearest friends,
Donna and Janet

Rascal

Prologue

The Chester County courtroom was packed—
men, women, and children scrunched together
on long wooden benches, craning their necks to
get a better look at the handsome, dark-haired
defendant.

"He don't look so high-and-mighty now," one
woman whispered.

"Let's see you whip out that guitar now,"
another taunted. "'Lotta good it'll do you *here*,
big shot."

"Order in the court!" The black-cloaked judge
slammed his gavel hard enough to make them
all jump. "Order in the court!"

Outside, photographers lined the corridors,
poised and ready for the moment the verdict
was announced and the heavy wooden doors
swung open. The lawn surrounding the courthouse was littered with people, some of them
having arrived to claim a spot early that morning, despite the rain that had fallen steadily for
two days and turned the grounds to slush.
Umbrellas formed a myriad of tiny colorful can-

opies, bright against a sky in which storm clouds
still scuttled and threatened to dump heavier
rain. Those without umbrellas clutched soggy
newspapers or sheets of plastic over their heads.
All of Chester was there—but then they knew
they'd better be if they wanted to keep their
jobs at the metal fabricating plant where Sam
Prichard reigned supreme. Sam signed their
paychecks and had signed their parents' paychecks before that. And Sam's granddaughter,
Becky, had been disgraced.

The judge cleared his throat. His face was as
somber as the late April sky outside. "Will the
defendant and his counsel please rise and ap-
proach the bench."

Deacon Brody stood, his tall frame dwarfing
that of his lawyer. Dressed in a dark blue Perry
Ellis suit, he looked subdued. There was little
resemblance between this man and the country-
western star who'd entertained some of these
same people in a Nashville auditorium more
than a year ago.

One reporter had written of that performance:
"Deacon Brody stomps and shimmies and gy-
rates across the stage, his chiseled features
contorted beneath a mane of blue-black hair,
as though performing unnatural sex acts. He
plays his fiddle at a manic pace that grips the
audience and leaves them exhausted and emotionally drained. A musical virtuoso, Deacon
moves easily from guitar to fiddle to piano,
courting his audience with a deep, gritty voice
that is too rough around the edges to sound
pretty but sensual enough to melt the most
hardened soul."

Little did anyone know it would be Deacon's
last performance.

Gone now were the six-inch ponytail, the flashy western-cut shirts, and the skintight jeans that had been tagged obscene by a religious group bent on boycotting the sale of his records. His exotic eel-skin boots had been replaced by leather oxfords. Even his earring was absent, the small gold-nugget cross he always wore in his left ear. He looked as respectable as a seminary student on his way to a Bible study class.

The judge cleared his throat and shuffled the papers before him. From time to time his gaze wavered across the courtroom to where Sam Prichard sat.

"Deacon Brody, the jury finds you guilty of the charge of soliciting a minor. The court hereby sentences you to two years of probation and five-hundred hours of community service work." He paused. "Do you have any questions?"

Deacon and his lawyer exchanged looks of relief. They had been expecting a prison sentence up until the last minute, when, through a lot of wheeling and dealing and coldhearted cash, they'd been able to persuade the prosecutor to go for a lesser charge. The legal system in Chester stunk as bad as the smell coming from Sam Prichard's fabricating plant. Everybody knew it. Still, his lawyer had advised, it wasn't a stroll in the park trying to prove statutory rape when the girl in question looked twenty-three and had been sneaking into honkytonks since she was twelve. They could appeal. With a little luck, they might win. But it wasn't a risk Deacon was prepared to take. He'd already lost a year of his life. Why continue fighting it when he could simply sweeten the pot for a few people and get out of it? His lawyer stepped forward a fraction. "Your honor, in anticipation of this sentence, my client would like permission to return to his hometown of Calgary, North Carolina, to carry out these orders."

The judge nodded. It was obvious he didn't want the likes of Deacon Brody in Chester any more than the man himself wanted to be there. "Very well. I'll see that a transmittal is processed immediately. This court is adjourned." He slammed his gavel again. As before, several onlookers jumped.

Deacon didn't hear the explosion of courtroom emotions as he dully watched the judge exit the room to his private chambers. Nor did he notice the way his band members tried to block the rush of photographers who swept through the double doors in pursuit of him.

He was too wounded to see anything but his own pain and bitterness.

One

"Well, I, for one, wouldn't let the man within fifty yards of my daughter," Maybelline Carter said with much aplomb.

"You don't even have a daughter, Maybelline," Ailene Jensen said with a snort.

Cody Sherwood Cox tried to stifle the yawn that had been tugging at her bottom lip for the last half hour as she served yet another cup of coffee to the ladies of the Calgary Garden Club. Their lively chatter competed with a sputtering air conditioner that put out more noise than cool air, and Cody now regretted spending thirty dollars on a new hairstyle when she should have used the money to repair the machine. The short brown bob that had looked so chic the day before at Nettie's Beauty Shop was as limp now as a discarded prom dress, having fought and lost the battle with the spring humidity. As had the wilted cotton blouse that had been so crisp when she'd put it on that morning, and the half slip beneath her skirt that clung to her thighs now like cellophane.

Maybelline paused as Cody emptied the ash-tray beside her. "What do you think, Cody dear?" she asked.

Startled from her thoughts, Cody glanced up quickly, then fixed her brown eyes on the woman. "I'm sorry, I wasn't listening to the conversation. What were you discussing?"

"We were talking about that rascal, Deacon Brody," Ailene said. "You know, the boy who jilted you all those years ago and ran off to Nashville to become a country-western star. Only he ain't a boy no more."

Another woman patted Cody on the arm. "If you ask me, he did you a favor runnin' off like that. He's a bad'un, that Deacon Brody. Always has been. And now this business with that fifteen-year-old girl." She clucked her tongue. "Frankly, you were smart to marry that Henry Cox fellow from Durham, even if it didn't work out. It's a whole lot easier bein' divorced than havin' to hang your head in shame over some-thin' like this."

Cody could think of about six dozen topics she'd rather discuss at the moment than Dea-con Brody. It still hurt to think of him. She had married, borne a child, divorced, and buried her parents within a year of one another, but none of those events had remained with her as deeply as the night she had walked out of Deacon Brody's life thirteen years before. She could still recall Eileen Brody's words.

"Do you love my son enough to let him go?"

Cody had discovered she did.

She had said good-bye and walked away from the most important person in her life. Of course, everyone, including her parents, assumed Dea-con had dumped her in the name of fame and fortune, and Cody had not bothered to tell them otherwise. What did it matter? A person did not care about pride when her heart was broken and her life shattered. She had simply packed herself off to Duke University right away and hoped for the best.

She had met and married Henry Cox at a time when she'd needed a friend desperately. And although the marriage had only lasted four years, their friendship had continued. He was wonderful to her daughter, Katie, and that's what mattered.

She'd thought all along that she'd gotten over Deacon Brody. Then, one day, little more than a year earlier, she had picked up the *Gazette* and found him staring back at her from the front page, beneath headlines too awful to imagine: COUNTRY SINGER JAILED ON SEX CHARGES.

She hadn't believed it then, and she didn't believe it now. All she could think of at the time was how good the years had been to him, despite rumors of a wild lifestyle, of parties that lasted all night. At thirty-two, he still had the power to take her breath away. Hers and a million other red-blooded women, she thought dully.

Cody realized suddenly that the garden club ladies had grown quiet. All eyes were on her. She glanced around at the looks of expectancy on their faces. "I read about the whole thing," she said after a moment. "Frankly, I believe Deacon was the real victim. After all, they say the girl was no stranger to honky-tonks," she added, "and that she'd been in one scrape after another. Maybe her family wanted to get her off their hands and secure her future at the same time."

Maybelline shook her head, and her eyes rolled in their sockets like marbles gone haywire. "Oh, Cody, how can you possibly defend a man who tossed you aside like week-old garbage, then ran off to Nashville and shacked up with a woman his mother's age?" She paused and drew herself up tightly, which wasn't easy for a woman her size. "I swear, sometimes you can be so naive."

A soft murmur ran through the group, and the women nodded in agreement. Cody leveled her gaze on Maybelline. She didn't appreciate being called naive. She'd grown up a lot in the past year and a half, what with losing both parents. It wasn't easy trying to run a business, keep her rental units in repair, and raise a spirited twelve-year-old daughter at the same time, a daughter who was already forty-five minutes late coming home from school. That thought drew a frown of concern from her. She had given Katie explicit instructions to come straight home so she could assist in preparing the food for the wedding reception that was going to be held in less than four hours. Four hours!

But first she had to set Maybelline straight. "I believe Mr. Brody was set up. Framed. Nothing is going to convince me otherwise."

"Oh, pssshaw!" Maybelline said, waving the statement aside. "Deacon Brody is trouble with a capital *T*, Cody, and everybody in town knows it! Why, have you forgotten that I was the assistant principal of Calgary High when you and that boy were an *item*? He was a handful then, let me tell you. Spent more time in my office than he did in his classroom."

Cody ignored the remark. She had seen a

side of Deacon that most people hadn't. A side that was too personal to discuss in front of these women. And she knew in her heart that Deacon would never lay a hand on a young girl. He had a soft spot in his heart for them, and she knew why. But it wasn't likely that Maybelline and her cohorts would agree, so she merely shrugged and began clearing the coffee table of empty cups, hoping the women would take a hint and leave.

"Why didn't he get a prison term for his crime?" Ailene Jensen asked as Cody made for the kitchen.

Maybelline folded her plump arms across her breasts. "'Cause he plea-bargained, m'dear, and got a lesser sentence. And 'cause he's so stinkin' rich that he could buy his way inside the Pearly Gates if he wanted." She paused, sucked in her breath, and her chest rose like a child's float taking in air. "So the judge gave him probation and community service work. If you ask me, they should have locked him up and thrown away the key. Instead, they said he could come back to Calgary to perform the work."

"I think it's a crying shame he's allowed to come back home and bring his shame with him," another woman said. "Especially since he was too good to play at our bluegrass festival a few years back."

A sudden ruckus made the ladies jump. They glanced around and saw that Cody had almost dropped the cups and saucers she was carrying. "I'm sorry," she said, getting a grip on the dishes. "Did you say Deacon is coming back to Calgary?"

Maybelline snorted. Her fleshy cheeks were pink from the heat. "Of course he's coming back," she said. "Why do you think folks are in such a panic? He could already be here, for all we know."

Patsy Barker cleared her throat and spoke for the first time. In a hushed voice, she said, "I'm just glad I have sons," she said, "instead of daughters."

The group nodded soberly.

Still reeling from the news, Cody pushed through the swinging doors that led into the kitchen. She set the dishes in the sink with a clatter and sank onto a chair, feeling as weak as a new kitten. Deacon Brody was coming home after all these years. She felt something close around her heart and squeeze. An intense longing? A deadly fear? What was she going to do now?

She had no choice. She and Katie would simply have to lay low until he finished his business and returned to Memphis. She wouldn't be able to draw a breath of relief until then.

Deacon Brody studied the odd looking structure with its pink imbricated shingle siding and wondered why Jim and Abigail Sherwood had painted their house pink to begin with. It had been that way for as long as he remembered. Still, the gargantuan Victorian was impressive, with its turrets and steeply pitched roof. The property surrounding it ran a full city block and was protected by a six-foot wrought-iron gate and tall red-tipped hedges. He knew it well. Many was the time he'd scaled that very fence, then climbed the back trellis to Cody's bedroom window. The two of them would sit on the roof and kiss and watch the sun come up. Then they'd kiss some more. Of course, it had never occurred to them they might fall and break a bone, or worse, their necks. The only thing they'd worried about was getting caught by Cody's parents, who had guarded her as though she'd belonged in a sealed vault at Tiffany's. He suspected they'd been overprotective due to their ages. Abigail Sherwood had suffered two miscarriages before she'd given birth to Cody at the ripe age of forty-four.

Deacon continued to pace the walk, just as he'd done the previous evening, before he'd finally given up and driven to the Palm Court Motel. The sign in the window beckoned him. APARTMENT FOR RENT. INQUIRE WITHIN. He grunted. Cody's family must've fallen on hard times to have to chop the place up into apartments and rent them out to strangers. The thought pleased him more than he cared to admit. Thirteen years was a long time to hold a grudge, he told himself. Besides, he needed a place to stay, and the good folks in Calgary hadn't exactly received him with open arms. And it wasn't as if he posed a threat to the Sherwoods' daughter anymore. Cody probably had a whole slew of kids by now.

Where else could he go?

With a sigh of resignation, Deacon took the steps slowly and paused before the front door to knock.

Dressed in a white apron and sporting a nylon hair net that would have been the envy of grandmothers everywhere, Cody tasted one of the individual seafood quiches she planned to serve at the reception. She waited for Katie to do the same. "Do you think they'll suspect it's imitation crabmeat?" Cody asked, having had to use an inexpensive substitute as she often did when she was forced to pinch pennies, something she found she did a lot of these days.

Katie shook her head. She was the spit and image of her mother, short brown hair and all. At the moment, her hair was disheveled, and the eye makeup she wore seemed more appropriate for a cocktail waitress. Cody knew she had been experimenting with her friends in the girls' bathroom at school again. She simply hadn't sent her up to wash it off yet. "I can't tell the difference."

Cody was about to answer when the doorbell rang. "Oh, I hope that's the champagne," she said. She hurried to the swinging door that led from the kitchen. "Go ahead and pull out the cheese trays," she called over her shoulder. "When I get back we'll cut up the raw vegetables." Katie nodded as she swept through the door, but Cody didn't miss the look of bored resentment on her face. Although the girl was a big help at times like this, Cody knew she found the tasks dull, which meant she didn't want to spend the time necessary to do them right. Cody was often forced to finish them for her. One day she would hire help, she promised herself. One day her daughter would be able to spend time with friends and not have to do so much for the business. One day, when money was not so tight.

Cody hurried out of the kitchen and through the impressive dining room where a florist had just delivered a gigantic centerpiece of fresh flowers for the soon-to-arrive wedding party. Stepping out into the main hall that separated her private rooms from the rental units, Cody threw open the beveled-glass front door. "I hope you've brought plenty of champagne," she said. She took one look at the man on the other side, and her heart slammed to her throat. "Oh my," she said. "You're not from the liquor store."

Two

Deacon felt as though someone had hit him squarely in the face with a frying pan. At first he was too stunned to say anything. Both of them were. So they simply stood there and stared with their mouths agape.

He's grown taller, she thought.

She's filled out, he thought, at the same time hating himself for noticing.

The tabloids didn't do him justice.

Marriage and motherhood becomes her. She's still as pretty as she was in high school. Except for that thing, whatever it is, mashing down her hair.

I never really got over him.

I'll never forget how she hurt me.

This thought made his spine stiffen.

"Deacon?" The sound of her voice shattered the breathless silence and made them both jump as though a firecracker had been tossed at their feet.

He gazed back at her, feeling dumb and stupid and angry as hell for being there. What business did he have coming back to Calgary anyway? And what was he doing on Cody's front porch, for Pete's sake? Better yet, what was *she* doing there! Why wasn't she in Durham with her husband? He should've known something like this would happen.

"Hello, Cody." His voice was as cold and brittle as a frozen twig after an ice storm. "Are your parents in?" There now, he thought. It had come out sounding impersonal and business-like. No one would ever have guessed he had once loved her, that her touch had made his blood boil. Nobody would ever suspect he still held a grudge against her for what she'd done to him.

"My parents?" Cody blinked. Was this some kind of bad joke? she wondered. Then she realized he probably didn't keep tabs on what was going on in Calgary. "My parents died . . . a while ago," she said. The look on his face told her he hadn't known.

Deacon wanted to tell her he was sorry, but that was too personal, and he didn't want to get personal with her. He didn't even want to be there, and he knew that if he had half a brain, he'd march right back to his car, drive away, and never look back. Surely Cody had someone to look after the place, someone who rented the apartments out for her and saw to repairs. Surely he should be talking to someone else besides *her*. She probably had a nice Cape Cod in Durham and a husband who expected sup-per on the table by six. "I came about the apartment," he said instead, his voice neutral. "Is there somebody I should talk to about it?"

"The apartment?" Cody realized that she probably sounded dim-witted repeating everything he said. But she couldn't help it. She had not been prepared for the grown-up version of Deacon Brody. He was almost more than she could handle. Damn, but he looked good, all six and a half feet of him. She let her gaze take in his full length, from the tips of his boots to his head, where the raven-color hair curled past the collar of a western-style shirt. His chest was massive, his waist trim, his hips lean and muscled in a pair of shamefully tight denims. There had been enough written about his jeans and the buns they covered to wallpaper the local library. No, time had not been cruel to Deacon Brody. On the contrary, it looked as though time had played right into his hands.

Deacon unfolded the newspaper he held and pointed to the advertisement he'd circled in red. He was aware that she was staring. Let her look, he thought. He was used to women gawking at him as though he were nothing more than a hunk of meat. After having spent so many years on the road as an entertainer, he'd learned to take it in stride when women ogled him. He'd also learned there wasn't much a woman wouldn't do to get his attention, if she so desired. They had sent flowers, panty hose, garters, even underwear backstage in hopes of spending an evening alone with him. In the beginning, he'd gotten a kick out of it. Later, he'd found it dull. But Cody could look all she wanted. Maybe she'd realize once and for all what she'd given up.

"It says here you have a one-bedroom apartment for rent," he said. "And there's a sign in the window. Is it still vacant?"

Cody nodded quickly. "Yes, but why would *you* want to rent a room *here*?"

He glanced around once more, taking in the old-fashioned wicker furniture on the porch. It sagged slightly but looked inviting nevertheless, as did the bright red flowers growing in clay pots. It was a far cry from his sleek, modern-style mansion in Memphis, he told himself, but it would serve its purpose. Besides, he was bad news in Memphis and Nashville at the moment. "Is something wrong with the place?" he asked after a moment.

"No, of course not." Under any other circumstances Cody would have been thrilled at the prospect of renting the apartment. She could certainly use the money, and there wasn't a big demand for rental property in Calgary. But to rent to Deacon Brody, of all people! She would have to be out of her mind. She could not imagine him living in the same town as her, much less under the same roof! Not only that, she couldn't imagine him *wanting* to be there. And what about Katie? No, this wouldn't work at all. Every instinct she had told her to get rid of him fast, get him as far away as possible from her and everything that mattered. There were simply too many leftover feelings, too many things said that couldn't be taken back, too many things that should have been taken care of but weren't.

"I'm sure it's not what you're used to," she said matter-of-factly. "The kitchen is no bigger than a closet."

"I'm not much of a cook anyway, and you know how I like tight places."

Cody blushed. He knew all her buttons, and he probably wasn't going to waste any time pushing them. She was about to respond, when Katie pushed through the screen door. "Mom, the guy from the liquor store is on the phone and he says—" She came to an abrupt halt at the sight of Deacon. Her eyes looked as though they might pop right out of her head and roll across the porch. "Lord almighty, it's Deacon Brody!"

"Katie!"

The girl's face flamed a bright crimson. "Sorry, Mom, it slipped." She stepped closer to the dark-haired man. "You're Deacon Brody, aren't you? The country-western singer?" Her eyes bobbed in her head as she spoke, taking in his boots, his jeans, and the expensive sports car at the curb. "And that's a bloomin' Lotus you're driving, isn't it?"

Deacon nodded at the girl, a smile teasing the corners of his lips at her show of exuberance. She was a younger version of her mother. He'd met Cody when she wasn't much older than this girl, in fact. "Yes to both questions," he said, and the girl looked as though she might drop in a dead faint.

"Ohmygod!"

"Katie, get a grip!" Cody said, nudging her daughter, embarrassed at the display, and at the same time wanting to get her as far away from Deacon as she could. "What does the man from the liquor store want?"

"What man?" Katie blinked and pried her gaze off Deacon. "Oh, *that* man. He's two bottles short of the good champagne you ordered and wants to know if he can substitute a cheaper brand." Her eyes drifted back to Deacon. "I told him we didn't care if he delivered horse pee, just get here. But he wants me to check with you. Is Mr. Brody going to sing at the reception or something?"

"No." Cody waved the statement aside. "Tell the man from the liquor store I said it's okay. But I need that delivery immediately." Katie didn't so much as budge. "*Now*, please."

The girl sighed. "Yeah, yeah, yeah," she mumbled. "But I want Mr. Brody's autograph before he leaves." She disappeared inside.

"I'm sorry, Deacon," Cody told him. "My daughter is a bit . . . uh . . . spirited. Anyway, I'm in a state of panic this afternoon. Not only do we have rentals, we use the first floor of the house for meetings and receptions and such. We're expecting a group shortly. Now, what was I saying?"

She'd used the word *we* several times, he noticed, which meant her husband probably had a hand in the business as well. He couldn't help but wonder what kind of man she'd married.

"You were trying to make excuses as to why I shouldn't take the apartment," he said. His chest tightened at the thought. He didn't like this feeling of desperation, wondering where he was going to lay his head at night, wondering if the Clover Grill would refuse to serve him when it came time for his next meal. He never should have come back to Calgary. Fame and fortune meant nothing to these people. "But after seeing your daughter, I think I get the message loud and clear."

"My daughter?" Cody was suddenly anxious. "I don't understand what you mean."

The hard glint in his eyes only hinted at the anger and bitterness that had been with him for the past year. "Why don't you stop pussyfootin' around, Cody, and tell me the real reason you don't want me here." Her mouth fell open, but before she could respond, he stepped closer, so close, Cody could smell his after-shave, could see her own reflection in his black eyes. He didn't stop until the rock-hard muscles of his thighs pressed against her own.

"Why don't you come right out and tell me you don't want me under the same roof with your little girl? You're as bad as the rest of them. The least you could have done was be honest with me. Let me know where I stand." He pressed closer. She could feel his belt buckle nudging her stomach. Her pulse quickened. The look on his face told her he knew exactly what he was doing and what he was doing to her. "You obviously enjoy making a fool out of me. Well, congratulations, you succeeded. Again," he added. Without another word, he turned on his heels and stalked away, leaving her breathless and tingling where he'd touched her.

Cody watched in disbelief as he made his way toward his car. It took her a moment to realize what he was so angry about, and when she did, she felt relieved. Suddenly, she understood. "Deacon, wait," she called out. He ignored her. "Excuse me," she said a bit more firmly. She planted her hands on her hips when he refused to even acknowledge her. She may as well have been talking to the moon for all the notice he gave her. "Hey, I'm talking to you, Deacon Brody," she called out loudly. "You wait just a darn minute!"

His hand on the door handle, Deacon paused beside his car and glanced up at her as she almost flew down the steps, across the yard, and through the open gate separating them. She looked mad enough to spit. "Yeah, what?"

Cody came to an abrupt halt at the curb and glared at him. Standing beside the shiny car, he looked as though he'd just stepped out of a television commercial. He really was a handsome devil, she thought, but then he'd always been heaven to look at. And touch. She could still recall the texture of his skin . . . the back of his neck where the hair grew sparse . . . the leathery feel of his wide back. . . .

"Just who do you think you are?" she demanded, pushing her wayward thoughts aside. His gaze strayed to her heaving breasts, his eyes hard and penetrating. Cody felt naked and exposed, as though he had just torn her blouse open and branded her breasts with his hostile stare. She felt flushed and clammy at the same time. How did he manage to do these things to her without even touching her? Her anger mounted as she realized how much control he still had over her—if not over her life, at least over her senses. "You have no right to accuse me of . . . of being prejudiced against you. You, of all people, know what it's like to be judged unfairly."

He couldn't have been more surprised if she had taken a crowbar to his windshield. Deacon snatched his gaze from her breasts and raked his hands through his hair in confusion. "What the hell am I supposed to think?" he said. "You've made it plain you don't want to rent to me. After seeing your daughter, it doesn't take a genius to figure out why."

"Well, you're wrong. I simply feel the apartment is too small and not nearly as nice as you're used to. I don't think you'd be happy with it at all."

"I'm not a happy man at the moment. One

more inconvenience isn't going to matter. Besides, there are no other vacancies in town."

"I don't believe that. Did you try Crestwood Townhomes?"

"They said they're full up. I don't plan to hang around long enough for someone's lease to run out."

"Let me see your newspaper," she said, almost snatching it from his hands to keep from touching him. His arms were still lean and brown, she noticed, his hands big but nicely shaped with long, tapering fingers. He had been born to play music, and he'd started young, from the moment he could lift his daddy's old Gibson. He was self-taught because there'd never been money for lessons. Not only had he perfected a number of hymns on the old Wurlitzer at church, he could play a mean banjo as well. At twelve, he'd started sneaking out to a honky-tonk where he'd practiced with a group of jazz and blues musicians. Gazing at those fingers now, she remembered how they'd felt on her so long ago; stroking her breasts and thighs, tantalizing her senses.

Cody's stomach pitched at the sweet images. She attempted to study the listings he'd circled in red. It both frightened and annoyed her to know that she still found him so devastatingly attractive. At the same time it didn't surprise her. Hadn't she compared every man she'd met to him? And hadn't they all fallen short?

"You called all of these places?" she finally asked, taking care not to give her feelings away. This was not the eighteen-year-old boy she'd once loved, she told herself. This was not the same boy who'd wept when she'd ended their

relationship. Yet the memories remained painfully vivid.

"I've decided to go to Duke University after
all," she'd told him at the time. "I don't want us
to end up like your parents, living from hand to
mouth. I don't want to grow old before my time,
like your poor mother." It was a cruel thing to
say, she'd known, but she'd had to do it. For his
own good. She'd had to hurt him, make him
angry enough to walk away from her and never
look back.

Do you love him enough to let him go?

As long as she was alive, Cody would never
forget those words or the look on Eileen Brody's
face when she'd said them, only hours before
Cody had *lived* them. At eighteen, Cody had
found Deacon's mother a formidable opponent,
with her piercing black eyes and a brittleness
borne of pain and hard times, hard times that
had included the loss of a daughter to leukemia. Deacon's little sister. Eileen had hidden
that pain behind the wrong shade of makeup—
garish turquoise eye shadow that clashed with
the midnight blue mascara clumped together
on her stubby lashes. "My son could hit it big
one day with half a chance," she'd said.

"I believe he's going to be more famous than
Charlie Rich or Merle Haggard," Cody had replied.

Eileen's smile had been forced, drawing attention to the hot-pink lipstick that had bled
into the lines and cracks around her mouth.
"But we both know that isn't likely, don't we?
Now that he's graduated high school, there's a
job at the plant with his name on it."

Cody had almost winced at the thought of
Deacon pulling shifts at the local textile plant,

the same plant his father had worked in till the day he'd died. "It won't be forever," she'd replied. "Only until he makes a name for himself with his music." But she'd realized even as she said the words that men aged quickly in that plant.

"And what about you, Cody? Are you just going to walk away from that college education your parents have planned for you? I know kids who'd give up their right arms to go to Duke University."

It was not a subject Cody had wished to discuss. Although her parents had assumed she'd leave for college that fall, she'd had no intention of going anywhere without Deacon. She and Deacon had been merely biding their time until they could afford to get married, even if they had to elope. They'd grown tired of waiting. Once they had allowed themselves to go beyond petting, the situation had become tense. Jim and Abigail Sherwood had been anxious for Cody to go to Durham and acquaint herself with the town. They had friends she could stay with whose son attended Duke. It had all been conveniently laid out for her, and Cody had known why. Her parents had wanted her out of Calgary and as far away as possible from Deacon Brody.

"Deacon hates being poor," Eileen had said. "Poverty is what really killed his sister. We couldn't afford to take her to one of those fancy hospitals and have a specialist look at her. Deacon never forgave us for not having the money to save Kimberly. He'll end up hating you if you don't give him the chance to better himself." But when Cody had told him she planned to go to college after all, Deacon had insisted on going to Durham with her.

"You can't. My parents would never pay for my education if they knew we were still seeing each other. And I'm tired of sneaking around in order to be with you."

"You're ashamed of me." His voice had mirrored the hurt in his eyes, hurt that had quickly turned to anger. "I knew they'd get to you sooner or later," he had accused. "I'm not good enough for you—"

"Deacon, please—"

"That's it, isn't it? If my father had been a bank president or a lawyer, we wouldn't be having this conversation right now. If I hadn't been raised in a mill house, your parents would welcome me with open arms now."

"Can you blame them for wanting what's best for me?" she had asked

His look had turned hard, glassy, as though an invisible barrier had come down. She noted it now, frozen and impenetrable. It had not diminished in all those years.

"I called every last one of these places," he told her. "Same old story. No vacancy."

Cody folded the newspaper and gave it back to him, her lips pressed into a thin line of disgust. "I see." She understood clearly now, and it didn't sit right with her sense of fairness. All along she had suspected Deacon was the real victim in the yearlong court battle, but the folks in Calgary obviously didn't share that opinion. She folded her hands together primly in front of her. What was she about to do was sheer lunacy. Not only was it crazy, it was dangerous. But she couldn't very well turn her back on him now.

"I have three furnished rooms on the second floor. The rent is four hundred per month, including utilities. Unless, of course, you choose to run the air conditioner all the time. That'll cost extra."

He was so surprised, he didn't speak for a moment. Why would she be willing to rent to him when others were not? he wondered, then decided not to question his sudden stroke of luck. Maybe it meant things were beginning to turn around for him. "How 'bout I give you five hundred a month not to bug me about the air?"

"And I'll need a security deposit," she went on.

"No problem." He appreciated the fact that she was more concerned about him damaging her furniture than her daughter.

"I don't suppose you'll be entertaining women in your rooms at night," she said matter-of-factly.

The question caught him off guard. "Are you asking that as my landlady or out of simple female curiosity?"

Cody blushed. She'd read in the newspapers how cocky he could be. This was a side of him she'd never seen, but what could she expect when half the female population tittered and ogled him the minute they spied his handsome face on a glossy magazine cover? "I assure you I have no personal interest in your private life," she said. "I'm asking out of concern for a very impressionable twelve-year-old girl who lives here and pretty much knows everything that goes on. I ask all my single tenants to use discretion if they wish to . . . uh . . . have visitors." That wasn't exactly true. Ms. Vickers, the elderly tenant in number two, had never given her any reason to worry about something like that.

Deacon pondered it. It sounded good, but he didn't believe it for one minute. Well, not entirely. Something, male ego probably, convinced him she would have to wonder a little about his love life. She would probably flip if she knew how long he'd gone without a woman. That in itself probably had a lot to do with the fact that he'd caught himself staring at her legs twice since she'd come out onto the porch. But she could pretend all she wanted that her curiosity was based solely on some sense of propriety. And it did answer one question for him: She obviously lived on the premises.

"Tell me, is your husband as particular about what your tenants do behind closed doors?"

"I have no husband."

"That's not what I heard."

"I'm divorced."

"Oh." He was both surprised and curious, and it annoyed him to know he was even remotely interested in her personal life. "So what do *you* do when you meet a man you'd like to spend some quiet time with?" he asked. The question was way out of line and he knew it. But there was some deranged part of him that wanted to know.

Her voice was as crisp as a starched handkerchief when she spoke. "Look, I don't have time for this. In approximately ninety minutes, I am going to have one hundred people to feed. If you'd like to take a look at the apartment, I will show it to you. If not, then I'll have to say good-bye now."

He would not give her the pleasure of saying good-bye to him again. "Lead the way," he said.

Cody led him inside the entryway, where a large oval table rested, upon which several pieces of mail sat. "Katie and I live downstairs," she said. "We keep everything locked around here when we're not expecting anyone." She wondered how she was going to keep Katie away from him.

Deacon took it all in. "So I'll be dealing directly with you as far as the apartment is concerned?"

She met his look, and she wondered if she was reading more into it than he intended. "Is that going to be a problem?"

"Not at all." His tone was as convincing as the impersonal look he shot her. It gave nothing away, least of all the fact that he wasn't sure he could go through with the deal. Cody nodded, and he followed her up the staircase to the second floor, trying at all costs to keep his mind off the graceful sway of her hips and the gentle stirring in his belly. He concentrated instead on his surroundings. He'd never forgotten how big the house was. Still, it was homey and cozy. "How come you turned the place into an apartment building?" he asked.

"You mean other than the fact I needed the money?" She glanced down at him over one shoulder and smiled, but it was forced. "It had fallen into disrepair over the years, and when my parents died, I had a choice to sell it for less than it was really worth or spend the money to have it fixed up." She sighed. "I don't know, maybe I should have sold it after all. There's a lot of work involved in keeping the place up."

Deacon couldn't help but wonder what had put her in a financial bind. He'd always thought of her parents as having tons of money. Of course, where he'd come from the neighborhood bum had been better off financially. But what about that fine college man she'd married? Surely he was paying some kind of support for the kid.

Cody reached the top floor and stopped before one of the doors. She produced a key and slipped it into the lock, then pushed the door open and stepped aside so he could enter first. "It's clean and ready for occupancy," she said. "I supply fresh linens each week. There's a Laundromat down the street where you can wash your personal things." She crossed her arms and waited in silence while he looked around. The apartment had never seemed so small as it did now with him standing there, meeting her silent gaze with one of his own. What was he thinking? she wondered. Was he trying to come up with a polite way to tell her the apartment wasn't what he was looking for? She had known all along he wouldn't take it. Although it wasn't a bad little apartment, it didn't hold a candle to his place in Memphis. She had seen enough of his home on *Lifestyles of the Rich and Famous* to know that his prized Arabian horses had better living conditions than this apartment offered. But she'd owed him the chance to turn it down, no matter how hard it was on her emotionally.

Deacon studied the living room and its old-fashioned, overstuffed furniture, peeked into the galleylike kitchen, then walked into the bedroom. A mahogany four-poster bed and matching dresser had been polished until they shone like a new car. A small sitting area tucked in a turret gave the room a cozy, lived-in look.

"That bed is a family heirloom," Cody said

proudly from the doorway. Her furniture might not be as nice as his, she thought, but the memories attached to it were more meaningful. "I was conceived and born in it."

Deacon met her gaze across the silent room. He resented her divulging something so personal. Was she purposely trying to goad him? "And your own daughter?" he asked. "Was she conceived in this bed too?" He hated himself for asking. He didn't want to know. What he did know was that he would never be able to sleep in the same bed she had shared with another man.

Cody felt as though the air had been sucked from her lungs. "No," she said after a moment.

His relief was evidenced by the sudden relaxing of his jaw. "Then I'll take it."

Cody had not been prepared for his statement, and her surprise showed on her face. She panicked. "You will? Are you sure? I mean, perhaps you'd like to look around and see if you can find something a bit nicer." Oh Lord, what had she done! She paused and swallowed, but there wasn't a drop of saliva in her entire mouth. "Look, you don't want to rush into anything," she said quickly. "Maybe you'd like to look some more before you decide. Tell you what, I'll even hold the place twenty-four hours to give you time to decide."

She obviously didn't know how desperate he was, Deacon thought. He reached into his back pocket. "Is cash okay?"

"Uh, yeah, I guess so." Before she had time to consider what she was agreeing to, he handed her a wad of bills. She accepted it reluctantly, in exchange for the key she was holding. She was still reeling from the whole thing as she made her way to the door. She had been so certain he wouldn't take it. What had come over her? Why had she taken such a gamble? What was she going to do now! And what about Katie?

"Is there a coffeepot in the place?"

Cody stopped in her tracks. "A coffeepot?" Somehow, she couldn't imagine him as a coffee drinker. She could see him swilling beer and eating pretzels, but never sipping something as tame as coffee. "There's an electric percolator beneath the sink." She edged closer to the door. She was trembling now. She needed to be alone. She needed to sort through what she had done and consider the possible consequences.

"I really have to go," she said, her voice shaking as badly as the rest of her. She had to separate herself from the man and the feelings he evoked. "If you need anything, just let me know." She paused briefly. "And I would appreciate it if you could carry in your belongings before my guests arrive." She left him then and hurried down the stairs, tucking the cash in her bra. It was the safest place, she knew—no one had looked there in years. "What am I going to do now?" she muttered under her breath.

When Cody entered the kitchen a moment later, she found Katie on the telephone talking ninety miles per hour about meeting Deacon Brody. And when she told her daughter the man was actually moving in, she thought she would surely have to perform mouth-to-mouth resuscitation to get the girl breathing normally again.

"He's moving upstairs?" Katie said in a voice that was so squeaky Cody thought of going for the oilcan. "Why would *he* want to live *here*, for Pete's sake?" she asked, glancing around the

kitchen as though there must've been something spectacular about the place she'd over-
looked.

"Well, it's not *that* bad," Cody said, feeling the
need to defend their home. The girl merely
gawked back at her, remaining as still as a
mannequin. Finally, Cody clapped her hands
together, and Katie jumped as though she'd
just come out of a deep sleep. The girl wouldn't
be worth a flip for the rest of the day. "Okay
now, back to work," she said. "We've got a
million things to do." She washed her hands at
the sink and dried them on a towel. "Now,
where did I put my hair net?" she said, search-
ing for the tacky net she always wore when she
personally saw to the food preparations.

Katie was still walking around in a daze.
"You're wearing it."

The color drained from Cody's face. "No," she
whispered, a sense of dread washing over her.
She was scared to touch her hair and see for
herself. "Please tell me I'm not. Not in front of
him!"

Katie suddenly seemed to come out of her
hypnotic state and realize what was going on
around her, including her mother's mortifica-
tion and the pea-green tint it had cast over her
face. The girl collapsed into a fit of giggles.

By eleven o'clock, the party had wound down.
Cody saw the last of the stragglers out the door,
put the leftover food away, and said good night
to Katie. Finally, she decided to step out on the
front porch for a breath of fresh air before turning
in. She was too jittery to sleep after what had
been a day of surprises. First she'd learned

Deacon Brody was back in town, then before she'd had time to even digest the information, she'd opened her front door and, lo and behold, there he'd been! It would have seemed too much of a coincidence if it hadn't happened to her, but this was just her sort of dumb luck.

Cody pushed through the heavy wooden door and stepped out onto the porch in her stocking feet, having already kicked off her high heels. She didn't bother with the porch light, knowing it would draw gnats from every direction. She closed the door softly behind her and started across the porch.

"So you decided to join me," a male voice said.

The sound scared Cody so badly she almost tripped over her own feet. Fortunately, she quickly recognized him. "Deacon, what are you doing out here?" she asked in surprise. She could barely make out his silhouette in the moonlight as she walked closer.

"Sitting here watching the last of your guests leave. Sorry if I scared you."

"Oh, well . . ." She didn't really know what to say. Should she stay or go back inside? she wondered, knowing she might appear rude if she chose the latter option. But common sense told her she had no business being there, sharing the moon and stars with this man. She reached for the door. "Well, good night," she said.

"Don't leave on my account," he said.

She paused with her fingers on the door handle. "I thought maybe you'd appreciate a little privacy."

"Please." He indicated the chair next to him. "People have been avoiding me since I hit town."

She nodded, closed the distance between

them, and sat. "That'll all blow over soon," she said, although she wasn't as convinced as she sounded. He shrugged, and she could tell it was not a subject he wished to pursue. Instead, he took in the cream-color chemise she wore.

"You're all gussied up tonight." He liked her outfit. It was simple and unassuming, a pleasant change from the flashy clothes he was used to seeing on women in show business.

Cody smiled and fidgeted with her collar unnecessarily. "I have to dress up for these events." She paused and shot him a sidelong glance. "I'm surprised you recognized me this afternoon, wearing that hairnet."

"I'll have to say, this is an improvement," he told her, noting the short, wavy hairstyle that flattered an already attractive face. But then, she'd always been pretty. In high school, she'd been one of the prettiest and most popular girls around. Which had made him wonder what she saw in him, a nobody. Now he wondered if maybe she wasn't trying to fish for compliments. Women were good at that sort of thing, he knew. They liked to point out some tiny, minuscule flaw, then let a man trip all over himself minimizing it and bringing to mind their strong points. The trouble was, she had more strong points than he cared to name.

He decided to change the subject. "I was just remembering when I used to sit out on the front porch at night as a kid," he said after a moment. "I've gazed up at many a sky just like this one from the front porch of my parents' house. 'Course, our place wasn't as nice as this," he added, thinking out loud.

Cody knew how much Deacon had hated being poor. Not because he was enamored of material things, but because he hadn't liked to see his family do without. Now he provided well for them. He'd seen to his brothers' educations and had set his mother up in a fancy retirement home. "Well, you've certainly made up for it with that place of yours in Memphis," she said after a moment, trying to make her voice sound light despite the tension between them. "I've seen pictures of it. It's gorgeous."

Deacon was glad she'd seen a picture of his place. He wanted her to know, without a doubt, that he'd made it big.

"You've come a long way, Deacon," she said softly. "You should be proud of yourself." She wondered if his mother was proud.

Deacon studied her in the dim light. She sounded sincere but not overly impressed. He wondered if she resented his fame, if maybe she wished she'd taken a chance on him after all. Instead, she'd dumped him and married someone else. A college guy. He had never been college material. His grades hadn't been good enough. But then, he'd had to work full-time during his high school years, so there hadn't been much time for studying. He couldn't help but wonder why Cody had divorced, or if she still cared for her ex-husband. But that was none of his business, so he shoved the thoughts aside. "How old is your daughter?" he asked after a moment.

Cody shifted in her chair. Why was he suddenly so interested in Katie? "Twelve."

He nodded. "She looks just like you."

She relaxed. "Yes, I think so too."

"Does she see her father often?"

"No." Cody clasped her hands together in her

lap. She did not want to discuss Katie *or* her ex-husband with him. "By the way, I forgot to ask about your mother. How is she?"

He shrugged. "Okay, I guess. I spent a few days with her before I came here. I've got her in a nice place right outside of Memphis. One of my brothers is helping me look after her." He paused. "Listen, about this afternoon." He paused again, knowing he had to set things right with her. He'd acted like a jerk earlier, stomping off, accusing her of being like the other gossips in town. She hadn't deserved it, especially since she'd been kind enough to open her doors to him. No matter how she had hurt him personally, he knew she was fair about most things. "I'm sorry I jumped to the wrong conclusions about the apartment. I've had folks slamming doors in my face for two days now, so I just thought—"

"There's no need to apologize. I understand."

He regarded her. "I haven't been easy to get along with these days. This whole court thing has been more than I can stand. I think if I wasn't so afraid of dying, I would have ended it all by now." The confession startled him as much as it did her. He had not realized until this very moment how deeply the ordeal had affected him. It had dragged him so far down emotionally that he was beginning to wonder if he would ever recover.

Cody felt her heart turn over in her chest. "I'm sorry, Deacon." And she was. She had problems, but none so bad that she would consider ending her life. Losing her parents within a year of each other had taught her how fragile life was, how precious each moment. With very little money left over to enjoy the finer things in life, she had learned to appreciate the little ones: spring flowers, summer rain, Katie's laughter. Even her money problems seemed insignificant when she considered the joys in her life.

Deacon shrugged again. It was odd that he could still talk to her so easily, but then she had always been a good listener. Except, of course, for that one time when she had refused to listen to reason, when she had insisted that her education was suddenly more important to her than anything else—including him. But that was all behind them. The only thing that mattered now was their being civil to each other.

"It's all my fault," he said, thinking out loud.

Cody snapped her head up. "What is?"

"This whole damn mess." He buried his face in his hands and shook his head. When he raised up, his expression was grim. "I should have used better judgment at the time." He stood, shoved his hands deep into his pockets, and walked to the edge of the porch. He had wanted to talk about his case for a long time, but hadn't. Not only had his lawyer advised him against it during the trial, he'd warned him not to say anything afterward that might find its way into the newspapers or tabloids. Instead, he had kept it all inside until it had festered into a painful wound.

"Deacon, for what it's worth, I don't believe you're guilty for a minute."

He regarded her. It meant a lot to him to know she believed in his innocence, although he wasn't sure why. "What makes you so sure?"

"Because I know the kind of man you are. And I know you have a soft spot for girls. I remember when I used to baby-sit little Amy Johnson and you'd drop by. It was all I could do to get her to bed. She'd sit in your lap for hours listening to your stories." She paused. "I know you never quite got over losing your sister, and I know deep in my heart that you'd never lay a hand on a little girl." She saw his jaw harden at the mention of his sister, and she knew she'd touched a sore spot.

Finally, he chuckled. "Where were you when my lawyer was trying to find character witnesses?" he asked.

"I would've been only too happy to come if you'd asked."

He pondered it. "I'm not sure it would have done any good. The evidence was pretty incriminating." He clasped his hands together and leaned against the railing, remembering the events that had led to his trial. "Some of the guys in my band had had too much to drink that night. Our business manager had learned we'd been nominated for another Grammy for our song 'To Hell and Back for a Blue-Eyed Woman.' Instead of driving back to Memphis after the performance as we'd planned, we stopped off in this little one-horse town for a room, and a couple of the guys ended up partying till dawn. I remember waking up when I heard something break in the adjoining room. When I went to investigate, I saw the girl they accused me of debauching. She may have fooled everyone else into thinking she was old enough, but she didn't fool me. I could tell she was just a kid. Anyway, I told one of my band members to take her home, but when it came time for him to testify on my behalf, he didn't remember. 'Course, he was drunk out of his mind at the time. I should have escorted the girl out myself. But I had been nursing a cold for three days, and the medicine I'd taken had made me groggy. I went back to bed and didn't so much as turn over the rest of the night."

"I read they found her in your bed."

He nodded. "The next morning I woke up and she was lying naked next to me, and there were a couple of hillbillies holding shotguns to my head."

"How'd they get in?"

"Hell if I know. But there they were, each of them holding a barrel to one nostril, telling me how I'd ruined their sister and how I was going to march my sorry butt up to the courthouse and marry her. And I answered something like 'When hell freezes over.'" He paused and chuckled. "That was not the right thing to say at that particular moment. They almost rearranged my face."

"So what happened?"

"Well, when they realized I wasn't going to make an honest woman out of their sister after all, they marched me up to the courthouse all right, but I ended up in a jail cell on the second floor. A couple of the deputies, who claimed to be the girl's cousins, beat the slop out of me, and the rest is history."

"Did it occur to you at the time that someone was trying to set you up?"

He laughed. "It looked fairly obvious to me."

"Why'd you plea-bargain?"

The smile faded. "Because they were going to put me behind bars for a long time, Cody. I'll tell you, that town is as crooked as they come.

Everybody is related to each other through blood or marriage. It cost me a fortune to get out of it."

"I can't believe something like that can happen in this day and age," she said. "Isn't there something you can do?"

He shook his head. "I just want to forget about it and get on with my life. And the next time I have to travel from Nashville to Memphis, I'm going by way of Pensacola, Florida." They both laughed, and he raked one hand through his hair. "Anyway, I don't know why I'm telling you all this, except sometimes I think I'll go crazy if I don't get it out."

"I'm glad you told me," she said. "I hope it helps."

He was silent for a moment. "Folks don't want me here. It was a mistake to come back."

Cody pondered it. "Well, can you blame them, Deacon?" At his look of surprise, she went on. "You were too busy to play at our bluegrass festival a few years back. The city had planned a big welcome party for you. Some people's feelings got hurt when you couldn't make it."

"I didn't find out about that until it was all said and done," he told her. "My manager handles my engagements, and he'd already set me up for a stint in Vegas. I wrote a letter of apology when I found out, but it was too late."

"I'm sure folks will get over it after a while," she said. "It just takes time."

He sighed. "In the meantime, I've got to meet with a Miss Alma Black first thing in the morning and get started on my community service work," he said.

"You'll get through this, Deacon," she said hopefully. "I've discovered that hard times only make us stronger." She stood, crossed the porch, and sat on the railing. "You'll get through this and be a better man for it, believe me."

"You sound like you talk from experience."

She shrugged. "Well, I went through a bad time with my father a few years back," she said. "He was sick for a couple of years before he died. The medical bills ate up his savings. Katie and I had to move back here to be close to him, because he insisted on dying at home. Then, just as I was getting over his death, my mother dropped dead of a heart attack. I thought I was going to lose my mind." She offered him a sad smile. "I think the only thing that kept me going was knowing I had to be strong for Katie. She has no one else but me."

"What about her father?"

Cody wasn't prepared for the question. She groped for a response. "Well, I've always been there for her," she said quickly. "I don't like to depend on others to help me with her."

He gazed down at her steadily, a half-smile tugging his lips. "Yes, you always were a stubborn little thing," he said. "I'm sorry you had to go through all that, Cody. I'm beginning to realize that I've been so wrapped up in my own problems that I hadn't noticed everybody around me has them as well." He felt bad for her, wondering how she had managed to weather it all. He wondered if she'd had anyone she could talk to at the time, someone who would just listen as she was doing for him right now. Part of him hated her for what she'd done to him, but another part couldn't abide human suffering. He touched her cheek with the palm of his hand. "I wish I could have been here for you."

She was clearly surprised by his touch, the

show of tenderness, and it almost brought tears to her eyes. His hand was big and warm and comforting. "It's okay now. "

Deacon continued to gaze at her, thinking she had never looked so pretty or desirable. He still felt something for her, something other than anger. "Cody?"

"Yes?"

"Don't ask me why, but I've been wanting to kiss you since you took off that silly hair net."

Too stunned to speak, Cody remained still. Her heart thundered in her chest as he stepped closer. Without taking his gaze from her face, Deacon slowly reached down and threaded his fingers through her short hair, grasping her scalp, massaging and stroking it until Cody felt it tingle in response. Something fluttered inside her. Whatever she might have expected from him, it wasn't this, but when he lowered his head, she closed her eyes and raised her lips to his.

His mouth was warm and nicely scented, his arms strong as they encircled her. Cody felt his tongue prod her lips open, and she received him eagerly. She had never forgotten the taste of him, the feel of his body against hers. He slipped his arms around her waist and pulled her to him, fitting the hard planes of his body against her soft ones. He exuded power and strength. He was no longer a young man of eighteen, but a mature man in his thirties who seemed well practiced in the art of kissing and touching. And Cody was luxuriating in those gifts.

But when Deacon raised his head, he looked anything but happy over what he'd done. He stepped back and wiped his mouth with his hand.

"I'm sorry I got carried away," he said. "I haven't been around many women lately, I'm afraid. If I spend too much time out here in the moonlight with you, I'm liable to embarrass us both." He sighed heavily and made his way toward the front door. "Good night, Cody."

Still reeling from his kiss, Cody could only nod in response.

Three

"Dammit to hell!"

Cody, in the process of getting Katie out the door and to school, jumped at hearing the commotion outside. She hurried out to the porch to see what it was about, her daughter right behind her. Deacon Brody paced the front yard angrily, cursing and carrying on and looking for all the world as though he were having some sort of fit. "What happened?" Cody demanded.

"My car!" He bellowed the words. "Look what they did to my car!"

Katie gasped out loud. "Jeeze Louise!"

Cody glanced at the Lotus sitting in the driveway where he'd parked it the night before. She sucked her breath in sharply at the sight. Someone had egged it, and from her vantage point she could see two of the tires had been slashed.

"I should've known something like this would happen," Deacon muttered between gritted teeth.

"What a bummer," Katie said, circling the car. Something in front caught her attention, and her mouth flew open in horror and disbelief.

Cody joined her daughter, coming to an abrupt halt when she spied the menacing blood-red letters on the windshield. The words CHILD MOLESTER glared back at her. "Oh my," she said.

Deacon kicked one of the tires with his boot, feeling the need to vent some of his anger before he exploded. "D'you believe it?" He slammed one fist into the other. "I'd give anything to know who did this."

Cody's voice was calm when she spoke to her daughter. "Katie, go to school."

The girl looked crestfallen. "Now?" It was obvious she wanted to hang around and see what was going to happen next.

"Yes, now. You're going to be late."

"But, Mom! What about Deacon's car?"

"We'll take care of it. Hurry up now, or you'll be late."

Katie shot her mother a look of pure, unadulterated resentment. "I never get to hang around when something exciting happens," she said. But when it was obvious her mother was in no mood to argue, she turned around and flounced down the sidewalk. Cody heard her grumbling from the next block. She looked at the windshield. This was exactly the sort of thing she did not want her daughter involved in.

"Deacon, you're going to have to call Sheriff Busby," she said as he continued to rant and rave.

The look he gave her told her he was afraid she was very close to losing her mind. "Sheriff Busby! Are you crazy? He's not going to do

anything about it except maybe congratulate
the person responsible."

"Sheriff Busby has mellowed over the years,
Deacon."

He shook his head sadly. "Do you have any
idea what this car cost me?"

"I imagine it's more expensive than even a
Cadillac," she said, and was awarded with a
dark look that told her she was way off. "No,
Deacon, I don't have a clue. Our little car dealer
in town hasn't had a Lotus on the lot in weeks.
But, if you're not going to call the sheriff, I will.
A crime took place on my property, and I'm not
going to put up with it."

Sheriff Reuben Busby mopped the back of his
neck with a frayed cotton handkerchief, hitched
his britches over his belly, and peered at Deacon
Brody. "Yeah, I heard you was comin' back," he
said without preamble. "When'd you hit town?"

Deacon gazed back at the man, remembering
the night he'd cited the owner of the local
honky-tonk for having a minor inside, namely
Deacon Brody. "Day before yesterday."

"And you're already in trouble, huh?" He
wiped his forehead, adjusted the brim of his
cap, and peered at Deacon through humor-
filled eyes. "Couldn't you have waited a few
months? I retire in the fall."

Cody stifled the urge to smile from her place
on the porch. She knew the sheriff was just
teasing Deacon, but his wit was totally lost on
the man at the moment.

"Mr. Brody isn't in trouble, Sheriff," she said,
coming down the steps. "His car was vandalized
during the night."

The big man swung his gaze in her direction, and his face parted in a big smile. "'Mornin', Cody," he said, putting a thumb and forefinger to the brim of his cap in greeting. "I didn't see you standing there. How's Katie?"

"Fine, thanks."

He stepped closer and grinned conspiratori-ally. "You know, I caught her jaywalking in town the other day, and I told her if she didn't start using the crosswalk, I was going to tan her hide." He chuckled. "She said I'd have to catch her first, and since I was fatter'n most anyone she knew, that wasn't likely." He chuckled again. "That girl's a handful, Cody. She's gonna give you gray hair 'fore your time."

"Yes, I know."

Deacon looked from one to the other as they talked. "Could you look at my car now, Sheriff?" he said, mustering as much politeness as he could under the circumstances.

"Just a minute, boy," Busby said, waving him aside. "You're going to have to tell that ex-husband of yours to come down here and put a hickory stick to her behind and make a believer outta her, or else find you a man who will. Someone who can take a firm hand to the girl. I gar-run-tee that'll straighten her out."

Cody blushed. It was bad enough that she hadn't had a date in months but worse that the whole town knew about it. "Sheriff, would you like a cup of coffee?"

"No, he doesn't want a cup of coffee," Deacon shot back impatiently, surprising them both. "He came to look at my car."

Sheriff Busby angled a glance at Deacon. "I see you still got a temper, boy."

"Damn right I do. Somebody made a mess out

of a hundred-thousand-dollar car, and you haven't so much as taken a look at it."

The sheriff shoved his cap high on his forehead and studied the car. "Well, I reckon if you're fool enough to spend that much money on a car, you ought to have the good sense to keep it in a garage at night."

Deacon had never felt so frustrated. "Are you saying it's my fault that someone egged my car and sliced the tires wide open?"

Finally, Cody spoke up. "Deacon, there's no sense taking your anger out on the sheriff. He's trying to help you. If you would just calm down."

Deacon ignored her. "Look, I have to be somewhere in forty-five minutes."

"You ain't goin' nowhere in that car, boy."

"That's obvious. And stop calling me boy."

Cody shook her head and went inside the house, tired of listening to the two fuss. Besides, if the sheriff needed to ask her any questions, he would call her out. She started cleaning up from the night before, taking her time because the only thing she had on the books that day was a tea for a group of ladies from the First Baptist Church. She only hoped Deacon and the sheriff would have long disappeared by then.

Twenty minutes later, Deacon knocked on her door, looking somewhat calmer. "Do you mind if I use your phone?" he asked. "I have to call a tow truck."

She stepped back to permit him in. "What did the sheriff say?"

"Oh, he took a couple of pictures and said he'd file a report. He thinks it was done by a bunch of kids. Said they'd probably start bragging about it in a couple of days and he'd find out." He shrugged. "I don't have much faith in that, though."

"Have you had coffee yet?" she asked. "I just made a fresh pot. There's a phone in the kitchen you can use."

He followed her through the dining area and the swinging doors leading into the kitchen. "You got a phone book?" he asked. "I need to call a garage too." He sighed heavily. "The sheriff was right. I should have had more sense than to leave the car outside like that."

Cody pointed to the telephone book as she poured him a cup of coffee. "You said you had an appointment."

"Yeah, with the community service coordinator. I'm already late. That should impress her." He checked the listing and dialed.

"Maybe I can give you a ride," she offered. "I have to go out anyway."

He wasn't listening. "Is this Haley's Garage?" he asked.

Cody shrugged and went about her business as he discussed his car problems with someone on the other end. She had worried all night how she would face him after the scene on the porch. Someone had certainly solved that problem for her. Deacon was obviously so caught up in the problems concerning his car, he wouldn't give their kiss a second thought. He hung up the telephone after a moment. "They can fix my car, but it'll take a few days. In the meantime, they don't have a loaner. Damn!"

"Look, I'll be glad to drive you—"

"What?" He suddenly looked amused. "You're going to provide taxi service for three days?"

"No, but I can take you where you need to go right now," she said.

"And what am I supposed to do tomorrow and the next day?"

Cody had had enough of his grumbling. "Listen, I don't give a hoot what you do tomorrow and the day after. I'm offering you a ride now, and if you didn't have such a chip on your shoulder, you'd accept it and be glad to have it."

Deacon was surprised by her outburst. "You think I have a chip on my shoulder?"

"If it was any bigger, you'd need a crane to lift it," she said matter-of-factly.

"Are you saying I should be happy with the predicament I'm in?"

"No, but all this moaning and complaining isn't going to help either."

He was stunned by her words. He took the coffee cup she offered and sipped it, watching her from over the rim. His gaze wandered to her lips, and something in his gut tightened as he remembered how she'd tasted the night before. He should have his head examined, he thought to himself, not only for kissing her but for liking it so much. "What would you do if you found yourself in my position?" he asked, trying to push the images aside—images of Cody in his arms, Cody bathed in moonlight, her scent mingling with that of the magnolia blossoms. "What if you woke up one day and discovered you no longer had the career you'd worked all your life for?"

"Your career isn't over. It has only been delayed."

"And that all your friends thought you were some kind of pervert?"

"I wouldn't consider them friends," she said.

"You've got an answer for everything, don't you?" He wondered if she'd have an answer for the persistent stirrings that had kept him awake the night before.

"No, I don't. But if I found myself in your situation, I would try to make the best of it."

"'Make the best of it'? When the whole world thinks I'm a child molester?" He slammed his coffee cup down, and the coffee sloshed onto the counter.

"Not everybody believes that. I certainly don't."

"Why are you sticking your neck out to help me?"

"Because I believe in you. I always have."

He stepped closer. His eyes glittered like chunks of black coal. "If you had believed in me, you never would have thrown away what we had. You said you were afraid of ending up tired and broken like my mother. You didn't have enough faith in me to know I would provide for you."

"That's not so. I never doubted you, and I don't doubt you now."

"Don't you?" His words were silky smooth, but tinged with something she couldn't quite put a name to. He closed the brief distance between them. "Don't you wonder if maybe you aren't wrong about me this time? Don't you think it's odd that so many people think I'm guilty? Can all those people be wrong?"

"You're exaggerating, Deacon. Not everyone believes you're guilty. And, no, I don't wonder if I'm wrong about you. If I had doubted you for even one moment, do you think I would have let you move in under the same roof with my daughter?"

"You don't know me anymore, Cody. I've changed."

"Not so much that I can't recognize you for the man I once knew."

"I was just a boy then. You'd be surprised how fast you grow up in the entertainment industry."

"Nothing would surprise me anymore."

"Oh yeah?" He reached up and stroked her cheek. It surprised him that he could be so gentle, given the volatile emotions churning inside of him. "Would it surprise you to know I still feel something for you?"

Cody's mouth fell open in response. Deacon seized the opportunity, hauling her roughly into his arms and planting a heated kiss on her lips. He thrust his tongue inside deeply, hungry for the taste of her. Cody's head swam, and she stumbled against him, but he caught her up tightly and held her against him. His hands were broad and warm as they caressed her back, moving down her spine, rounding both hips and capturing them firmly in his palms. He squeezed and ground his lower body against hers, leaving no doubt in Cody's mind of his arousal. The kiss deepened, and Cody was certain her knees would have buckled beneath her if he hadn't been holding her. Then, without warning, he released her, and it took everything she had to keep from sinking onto the linoleum floor.

His eyes were startlingly black. "See what you do to me? You still have the power to get to me after all these years. I may have hated you at times, but I never stopped wanting you."

Then he was gone, and the only sound in the room was her own frantic heartbeat.

• • •

Alma Black was a big, middle-aged woman with a no-nonsense attitude and practical shoes that made sucking noises when she walked. "Mr. Brody, I'm glad you could make it," she said, leading him into a cramped office where paperwork spilled from every nook and cranny. "You're ninety minutes late."

Deacon slid into the chair beside her desk, hiked one leg over a knee, and regarded the woman. "I had car trouble."

"Car trouble, huh?" She studied him. "Your phone out of order too?"

"Huh?"

"Your phone. You couldn't call and tell me you were going to be late?"

"I don't have a phone. I called the garage from my landlady's phone." He started to get up. "Look, I came as soon as I could. If this isn't convenient, I can come back another time."

"Stay where you are, Mr. Brody," she said without looking up. "My time is valuable. You probably find that hard to believe, you being a hotshot celebrity and all, but I have other clients who are just as important to me as you are."

Deacon studied her, and for a moment it looked as though he might laugh. His day had been so rotten thus far that he would have been almost disappointed had the lady turned out nice. After a moment, he laughed. "You're not a country-western fan, are you?"

"What makes you say that?"

"You're not trying to suck up to me. A lot of folks do, you know. Especially women." He gave her that cocky smile he was so famous for.

She raised her gaze to him and regarded him with about as much interest as she would cold noodles. "Save it, Mr. Brody, for someone who appreciates it. As for myself, I prefer classical music."

This time he grinned. Damned if she wasn't about the most ill-tempered woman he'd run into in this town, next to his old assistant principal from high school, Maybelline Carter. "You don't care much for me either, do you?"

"I think you have a chip on your shoulder."

"A chip?" He frowned. It was the second time he'd been told that in one day.

"Bad attitude." She shrugged. "But then, I see it all the time in this business, so you're no different from the rest."

He didn't like being classified as the typical Joe Blow off the street. "What kind of attitude *should* I have, Miss Black? I've been falsely accused of a crime. My career is shot to hell. My friends and business associates refuse to talk to me." He offered her a snort of a laugh. "And you think I have a bad attitude? What do you expect?"

"I think when you've been given a lemon you should make lemonade, Mr. Brody."

He wondered if he'd heard her right. "What's that supposed to mean?"

"I have a job for you."

"Doing what?"

"Singing."

His ears pricked. It hadn't occurred to him they would give him a job doing what he liked best. He had imagined himself painting government offices or sweeping endless hallways, but never this. He straightened in his chair. "Oh yeah? Where?"

"The hospital."

Every muscle in his body stiffened. "You mean Calgary General?"

"We only have one hospital, Mr. Brody. Anyway, I've talked with the administrator over there, and he agreed that it would be nice if you could entertain the patients. Even those in pediatrics."

"A child molester in the pediatric ward? They must be desperate."

"You would be supervised at all times, naturally." This drew a frown from him. "This is an excellent opportunity for you to show the world . . . well, you know."

"That I can be trusted around little children?"

"Yes."

He almost flinched. She would never know how much her honesty had hurt him. Still, it was better than having her pretend to believe in him and then seeing doubt in her eyes. He thought of the hospital where his sister had died and of the sick and injured children he'd had to see every time he'd visited. He thought of the bright lights that had deepened the lines of devastation on his mother's face, of the smell of disinfectant. And he knew he'd rather be in hell than have to go back there.

"Forget it. I'm not interested."

Alma looked surprised. "Is there any reason you *can't* do the job?"

"Yeah, because I don't want to."

Her lips thinned into lines of impatience. "I think you should consider it."

"I said I'm not interested. You can find something else for me to do."

Silence. Their gazes locked, and it was obvious there was a mental tug-of-war going on between them. "I went to a lot of trouble for you,

Mr. Brody. It wasn't easy convincing them. You could end up making things a lot harder on yourself by not cooperating."

"You're wrong, Miss Black. It can't get any worse than it is."

She gave him a knowing look. "We'll see about that."

Four

"But, Ms. Vickers, you can't be serious."

Cody stepped out into the hallway and regarded the frail woman before her. Aurora Vickers had been her first tenant after the renovation to the second floor of the house had been completed. Spry at eighty-one, Ms. Vickers had never caused a moment's trouble, kept her little apartment immaculate, and had never been late with her rent. Not only that, she'd been like a grandmother to Katie, nursing her colds with chicken soup she made from scratch. And now she was threatening to move out, all because of Deacon Brody.

"I wish you'd reconsider," Cody said now. "Mr. Brody won't be here long."

Things hadn't settled down since the man had swaggered onto Cody's porch several days before, inquiring about the apartment. The worst part, she'd discovered, was dealing with his frustration. That kiss in the kitchen two days before had merely been his way of lashing out, expelling the pain and outrage that simmered just below the surface. Cody suspected he was trying to come to terms with all that had happened, but her own emotions had been on a continuous roller coaster since he'd hit town. There were simply too many leftover feelings between them. She saw them each time she looked into his eyes. He tried to hide his emotions behind that hard glint, but once or twice she'd seen a look of vulnerability cross his face that was reminiscent of the Deacon she had once loved.

"I haven't slept in three nights," Ms. Vickers continued. "Ever since he moved in. Pacing all night long like a caged animal." She rolled her eyes heavenward. "I can't stand it."

"I'll talk to Mr. Brody and explain what a light sleeper you are, Ms. Vickers. I'm sure he has no idea he's keeping you awake at night."

"The ladies from my Bible study group refuse to meet at my place now," the woman said, fidgeting unnecessarily with her collar as she spoke. It didn't matter how hot it was or how high the humidity, Ms. Vickers's clothes were always fresh and crisp as a new soda cracker. "One of them has a young granddaughter who comes with her." She gave Cody one of her you-know-what-I-mean looks. She didn't have to elaborate; Cody fully understood.

"Ms. Vickers, has it ever occurred to you that Mr. Brody might be innocent of the crime he was charged with?" The woman stared back at her as though she'd just sprouted horns.

"But the evidence—"

"Was circumstantial. Besides, even if Mr. Brody *were* guilty, which I don't believe for one minute, he has been punished. Can we afford to go on blaming him forever?" Her tone became gentle. "It's easy to love those people we trust and understand, Ms. Vickers. The real test is opening our hearts to those who aren't so easy to love."

The woman looked unsure now. "I don't want to appear uncharitable," she said.

"Believe me, I would never have permitted him under the same roof with Katie if I thought he was guilty. Why don't you sleep on your decision, Ms. Vickers? Your rent isn't due for another two weeks, so there's no rush."

"Well, maybe I *should* give it some more thought," she said. Her fruity voice trembled with uncertainty.

"Is the old bag gonna split?" Katie asked when Cody walked through the door.

Cody shot her daughter a stern look. "Really, Katie, do you have to refer to Ms. Vickers as an old bag? She happens to be a very nice lady." She couldn't understand the girl bad-mouthing the elderly tenant. Katie had always treated her like a member of the family.

"If she was nice, she wouldn't be thinking of moving out on account of Deacon."

It was obvious Katie was hurt by the whole thing and obvious that she would defend Deacon to the end. She was always listening for his footsteps on the stairs and found an excuse to be in the hall whenever she suspected he was coming down. Cody didn't like it, of course, but she'd discovered she had very little control over her daughter where Deacon Brody was concerned. Now, sitting in the large, comfy chair with her legs swinging over one arm, Katie peered out the window, waiting for Deacon to appear in the battered cab that he'd been calling on for three days. He must tip Eustace McKenzie, the driver, well, Cody thought, because the man was always close when he needed him. And Deacon did need him, because he'd begun his community service work. For some reason he refused to discuss it, and Cody didn't press.

The telephone rang and Cody answered it. "Oh, Mrs. Brownlee," she said, putting on the professional voice she used for clients. "I'm so glad to hear from you. Everything is all set for your daughter's baby shower tomorrow afternoon. I even managed to make the baby booties the same color as the napkins and decorations." She paused as the woman on the other end of the line spoke. "What? You're canceling? Is something wrong?" She and Katie exchanged anxious glances. "But what about the food, Mrs. Brownlee? And all those baby booties?" After a moment, her voice became cool. "I see," she said. "Yes, Mrs. Brownlee, thank you for calling." She hung up.

"Another cancellation?" Katie asked.

"Yes. The second in three days."

"Did she say why?"

"She didn't have to. She's Maybelline Carter's sister, remember?"

"At least you have her deposit."

"I didn't charge Mrs. Brownlee a deposit." She sighed. "What am I going to do with all those *petits fours* I made to resemble baby booties?"

"Can't you freeze them?"

"They're lavender. Nobody orders lavender baby booties for their showers. It's always pink or blue. All that work for nothing."

"Ohmygod, it's him!" Katie sprang from the

chair as though someone had just stuck a hot wire to her behind.

"Who?" Cody asked, but she already knew.

"I'm going to check the mail," Katie said, rushing to the front door and throwing it open.

"The mail has already come."

But Katie wasn't listening. She bounded out the door and slammed it behind her.

Cody shook her head and went into the kitchen, where the miniature cakes she'd been working on so diligently the past two days sat on a tray on the kitchen table. Her little masterpieces. She wanted to hurl them against the wall. Then she wanted to tell Mrs. Brownlee where she could stick them all. Instead, she slumped in one of the chairs, picked up a bootie, and took a bite out of it. Her jaws stung with its sweetness. Maybe she'd eat the whole tray, she thought. What did it matter if she grew out of everything she owned and her face broke out? She had just about finished the bootie when she heard the front door open and close, then heard footsteps. The kitchen door swung inward, and Katie stepped through, with Deacon right behind her.

"Hi," Cody mumbled around a mouthful, feeling self-conscious as the dickens in a pair of old shorts and a T-shirt that advertised a barbecue restaurant in town. "Want a lavender baby bootie?"

"No thanks."

Cody knew she was staring, but heaven help her, she was incapable of doing anything else. Deacon epitomized masculinity in its rawest form in a snug tank top that emphasized his wide chest and shoulders, shoulders that rippled with each movement. His arms were lean and brown and corded with muscle. Veins bulged beneath his skin, and the sight made Cody's heart beat faster. His hands were planted squarely on hips that were encased in a pair of shamefully tight denims.

Startled by her own blatant perusal, Cody snatched her gaze away and made a production of dusting cake crumbs from her lap. "So?" she said, trying to appear casual. "What's up?" But it was not easy to sound casual when she feared her heart would literally burst from the adrenaline gushing through her. Lord, but he could make a woman itch in all the right places. How did he manage to look so good in old clothes when she herself looked like something the cat had dragged in?

"I just got my car back from the garage," he said.

"Great. How does it look?"

"Okay. I'm lucky the raw eggs didn't damage my paint job." He paused. "I was wondering if I could use your garage to park it in while I'm here."

"My garage?" She laughed. "Oh, Deacon, that garage is filthy. It's also crammed full of old furniture and junk," she added.

"I'll clean it out. Is there someplace else you can store everything?"

"How about the basement or attic?" Katie suggested, looking at Deacon with an expression that could only have been inspired by hero worship. "I'll help."

Cody arched both brows high on her head. For Katie to offer to raise her hands to do more than put food into her mouth or lift a phone to her ear was a momentous occasion. "Well, I have been meaning to get out there and clean it," she confessed. "I just haven't had time." She pursed her lips in irritation. Now that she'd had two cancellations, she had plenty of time on her hands. Cody reached for her purse and fumbled through for her keys. "Why don't we go out and have a look at it," she suggested. "When you see how much work there is to be done, you may want to back out."

He looked determined. "I can't afford to back out and have someone take another knife to my tires."

The three of them walked across the backyard to the detached garage that was the same pink shade as the house. Cody tried several keys before she located the one that fit. Deacon swung open the heavy wooden doors.

"Wow," he said.

Cody nodded. "I told you it was bad."

Katie took several steps back, as though half afraid the junk would come tumbling out and bury her alive. "I have to make a telephone call," she told them, and was out of there before either could stop her.

"Where did all this stuff come from?" Deacon asked, lifting the corner of a dusty bedspread so he could see what was beneath it. A battered dresser minus several knobs looked back at him forlornly.

"My parents were pack rats," she confessed, embarrassed. "They were afraid to throw anything away, in case someone needed it."

"Who would want this stuff?" Deacon said, lifting another spread and finding several mismatched kitchen chairs. As though suddenly realizing what he'd said, he flashed her an apologetic smile. "I didn't mean it the way it sounded."

But Cody was hurt nevertheless. "Not everyone can afford to furnish a mansion in Memphis with brand-new furniture, you know."

Now he looked embarrassed. "Yeah, well, I worked hard to get where I am, Cody. I shouldn't have to apologize for being rich."

"I don't expect an apology. But some folks would be glad to have this furniture."

He studied her. "You think my success has gone to my head, don't you?" he said, leaning against a tall chiffonier.

"Why should it matter to you what I think after all these years?"

"I'm not sure it does."

When she turned away, he reached out and grasped her by the wrist. His grip was strong and sure. "That's not true, Cody. It *does* matter what you think of me. You seem to be the only friend I have these days. I suppose I don't deserve it. I know I can be a real jerk at times." He paused and let her go. "Maybe I'm trying to test you."

"Test me?"

"To see if you're really going to stand behind me or turn your back on me the way everyone else has."

She didn't quite meet his gaze, but she was thankful when he released her. Unconsciously, she rubbed her wrist, where she still felt the heat of his touch. "I won't turn my back on you, Deacon. But at the same time, I'm not going to let you abuse our friendship."

"That's fair. But I want you to understand something, Cody: I haven't let money change what's important in my life. I mean, I appreciate what money can buy, but I'm also learning what money *can't* buy."

"Like what?"

"My innocence."

He glanced away, as though half afraid she might see something in his eyes he wasn't ready to share. Pain? Vulnerability? Cody wondered about it.

"I think, in this case, having money has hurt me. My *fans* don't even believe in me anymore. It's like they resent my success."

"Can you blame them, Deacon?" she asked gently. When he looked surprised, she went on. "Most of your fans are simple, hardworking people," she said, "who know they're going to have to struggle the rest of their lives to make a living. I think they were thrilled for you and your rags-to-riches success."

"But?"

"But look what you've become. Every time you pick up a newspaper there's a big story about how someone in your band got drunk and trashed a hotel suite or caused a fight in a restaurant."

"Cody, that happened once or twice early in my career. One of the guys in my band had a problem with drugs. When he refused to get treatment, I fired him. Besides, I always pay for any damage."

"And that makes it okay? What about the bad publicity you get as a result?"

"No, it doesn't, but we've mellowed since then."

"How about those extravagant parties you throw?" she said. "Most of us are living hand-to-mouth. How do you think your fans feel when they read about that villa you rent for five thousand dollars a day in the Virgin Islands?"

He thought about it. "Maybe I do it 'cause I'm so disappointed," he said after a moment.

"Disappointed?"

He nodded, then shoved his hands deep in his pockets. "I busted my butt all my life to get to this place called *success*, but when I got there I realized it wasn't at all what I was hoping for." When she looked doubtful, he went on. "I mean, sure, I live in a fancy place now and ride around in limos and eat at the best restaurants. On the outside it looks good. I *look* successful." He frowned. "On the inside, there's not much going on. I feel let down."

"Who let you down?"

"Maybe I let myself down."

She gazed at the thoughtful expression on his face, and for a moment he looked as unsure as the fifteen-year-old who'd walked up to her in school and offered to carry her books to class. She had been intrigued by the brooding, black-haired boy who always kept to himself. There was a raw look in his eyes, a maturity that stretched far beyond his years, a wisdom that came from too much pain. He'd been so different from her other friends. While she was involved in cheer-leading, the school yearbook, and various other clubs and activities, he did not participate in any of these. He didn't even attend football games, and he'd never once made the honor roll.

It wasn't until later that she learned he was trying to juggle a couple of part-time jobs after school to help his family. Deacon had had little time to enjoy being a teenager, Cody discovered. When he had had a couple of hours to spare, he'd practiced with his band.

But none of those things had mattered once he'd kissed her. From that day, Cody had arranged her schedule, her life, to fit his.

Deacon chuckled after a moment, interrupting her thoughts. "You'd make a good P.R. man, you know that?" He dropped his gaze to her breasts. "I mean woman."

"What makes you say that?"

"'Cause you're not like the people who work for me who always tell me exactly what they think I want to hear."

"Maybe they want you to keep them on the payroll." She went about lifting sheets off the old furniture to see what could be salvaged.

He nodded. "You'd be surprised how many so-called employees I have on the payroll. I've got a guy who makes a fortune keeping my cars clean and in good running condition. I pay another man doctor's wages just to travel with me, hang up my clothes, and tell me where I'm supposed to be and when." He chuckled. "He also makes sure I have chocolate milk in the refrigerator wherever I'm staying."

"Why do you do it?"

He grinned. "'Cause it eases the disappointment, makes me feel like a big shot, that's why. 'Cause I like having people take care of me and follow me around like a puppy." His smile faded. "And because I was forced to do the same thing myself once."

"You're talking about Mary-Lou Sly, aren't you?" She still remembered the first time she'd heard rumors surrounding him and the vintage country singer who'd helped him find success. Her morning sickness with Katie had escalated during that time, but she hadn't known whether it was caused by the baby, bad nerves, or both. She would rise each morning, her heart heavy with grief, her belly churning. She would be sick. So sick. Afterward, she would bathe her face with a cool cloth, and the tears would fall, and she would wonder if life would ever hold any happiness for her again. It wasn't until after Katie had been born that she'd decided she wanted to go on after all. Katie had given her a reason to live.

Deacon raised his gaze to her face. "Yeah, I'm talking about Mary-Lou. She was fairly big when I first arrived in Nashville, but she didn't start hitting the charts consistently until I began writing her songs. Which, I might add, I sold to her for peanuts. I didn't care who got credit for them as long as folks got to hear them on the radio. I was dumb as hell back then, I reckon. And I felt I owed Mary-Lou for giving me a job."

"You replaced her lead guitarist?"

He nodded. "The guy died of an overdose shortly after I hit town. Left a wife and little kids behind. I suppose that's one of the reasons I never messed with drugs." His look hardened. "Naturally, Mary-Lou screwed the poor widow out of every dime she owed her husband."

"Why do you say 'naturally'?"

"Mary-Lou wasn't what you'd call a kind woman. If she ever did a favor for anyone, she never let them forget it. I felt as if I owed her my soul before I got out." He gave a snort. "It never occurred to me how lucky *she* was to find someone at the last minute who could virtually pick up where her old guitarist had left off. I was practicing around the clock, surviving on four hours sleep at night. But all I could think of at the time was how lucky I was to be working for Mary-Lou Sly. And believe me, she never let me forget it."

Cody listened in silence, although most of what he was telling her was old news. The tabloids had had a field day covering his relationship with Mary-Lou, and Cody had been certain the emotional trauma would cost her the pregnancy before it was over. She almost hadn't believed it when Katie was born in perfect health. "You became her lover?" It was silly to ask. She already knew the answer.

"If you want to call it that."

She glanced away, because she didn't want him to see how much anguish the truth still caused her. She ran a finger across an old bookshelf where dust had gathered over the months. "I see."

Deacon didn't miss the look of pain that flashed across her face, despite the attempt she made to hide it. "Surely that doesn't bother you," he said, confused suddenly. Hell, she had already married Henry Cox by the time he'd moved in with Mary-Lou.

Cody swallowed. "No, of course not. I'm glad she was able to help you. Look what it did for your career."

He gave a snort of a laugh. "Only as much as Mary-Lou would allow," he said. "I didn't realize how insecure she was at the time. It took her two years before she'd even spotlight me in a show. Five years passed before she let me do a duet with her. I could do anything I wanted between the sheets, but let me try to steal some of her limelight, and she was ready to rake my eyes out with her guitar pick."

Her mind revolted at the thought of him and Mary-Lou Sly together. "Don't say any more, Deacon, please."

He snapped his head up at the sound of her voice. She looked pale. He stepped closer. "Does it bother you, Cody, to know that I was another woman's lover?"

"Of course it does." She refused to look at him, because she was near tears. "Isn't it enough that I had to see your affair in the headlines every time I picked up a newspaper or magazine? Why must you rub my nose in it? I don't *want* to know about what happened between the two of you, and I resent your bringing it up."

"Why should it have bothered you at all?" he asked. "You were happily married and pregnant at the time."

She laughed ruefully. "I suppose your mother was the one to deliver that news to you."

He frowned. "What's that supposed to mean? My mother was trying to protect me. She knew how broken up I was when you called everything off between us." He grabbed her upper arm and turned her around so that she was forced to look at him. "What do you think that did to me, Cody?" he demanded. "Knowing that you'd married someone else, knowing that another man was sharing your bed. Hell, I barely had time to get out of town before you found my replacement. I thought I'd go crazy when I heard."

"It was a small price to pay for what you've become," she said, her voice trembling as badly as the rest of her.

"And what have I become?" he demanded.

She glared at him. "A star, Deacon, a star! Isn't that what you always wanted?"

His own look was hostile. "Not if I had to do it without you." He shook her. "Why do you think it was so important for me to succeed, Cody?" When she didn't answer, he went on. "I wanted to be good enough for you, that's why. You were the first thing that ever came into my life that really mattered. You were the one who said I could go as far as I wanted in life. You believed in me when nobody else did. But then, at the last minute, you backed out." He released her. "You don't know what that was like, having all my supports pulled out from under me."

"It couldn't have hurt you too badly," she said. "You were able to find solace in Mary-Lou Sly's bed."

"You didn't do so badly yourself," he flung back at her. "I didn't even have time to unpack my guitar before you had a wedding ring on your finger and a baby in your belly. I've never seen a woman work that fast, Cody. Or maybe the two of you already had something going." The thought that she might have duped him when he'd been so smitten with her still managed to make him mad. "Tell me, were you sleeping with both of us at the same time?"

Cody raised her hand to slap him, but he was faster. He closed his fist around her wrist painfully. His gaze, clashing with hers, chilled her to the marrow. His voice was edged with steel when he spoke. "I wouldn't do that if I were you."

Cody just stared for a moment, feeling very close to tears. She was certain he had no idea how he'd hurt her by his cruel words. He had made a mockery of their times together, of the love they'd shared, of the memories she'd held near and dear to her heart for so long. She had fed on those memories for years, and they had nourished her soul and sustained her through her bleakest days. And now he was holding them up for ridicule and making them appear dirty and worthless, like setting a precious stone behind a grimy glass case in a pawnshop for all to see. Something inside her seemed to die. Her dreams?

"I think I could hate you," she whispered. When he didn't so much as flinch, she realized maybe he had changed after all. Irrevocably and forever, perhaps.

"Do you, Cody?" His voice was smooth as a satin sheet. "I wonder." He took a step closer, then another, until he was pressing against her. Cody took a step back, then realized she was trapped between him and a tall dresser. His thighs, hard and solid as concrete, held her tight against the furniture. She could feel the heat emanating from his body, seeping through denim and cotton, finding its way into the very pores of her body.

"Deacon, please." Her emotions were so torn, the words came out sounding like a whimper. She hated herself for sounding weak, hated him even more for making her that way.

"Please what?" he said. "Please come closer?" He ground his lower body against her, nestling his sex against her own femininity. "Do you hate this too, Cody?" He placed one palm against her breast and squeezed gently before seeking the nipple with a thumb and forefinger. He pinched and tugged it lightly, but the look on her face told him it had had a powerful effect on her.

Her body instantly came alive. Desire flared in her belly like quicksilver. She was hot and cold all at once. Flustered and confused. Nerve endings tingled below her skin's surface. The hairs along the back of her neck stood straight as flagpoles. And Deacon, damn his soul, was aware of the changes in her, she was sure of it.

His gaze remained fixed, his onyx pupils dilated. She watched her own metamorphosis in the blackness of his eyes. It was a cruel twist of fate that he had to be there at that moment and witness the changes in her when she realized the truth.

She was still in love with Deacon Brody. She still wanted the rascal, after all these years.

"You say you hate me, Cody, but I don't think you hate the things I do to you."

She was powerless to respond, powerless still when he captured her lips in a hungry kiss that was as delicious as it was mind-boggling. His tongue was greedy as he pushed past the seam of her lips, devouring the sweetness that waited inside. He slid one hand down the front of her slowly, singeing her skin through her blouse. Cody held her breath, then shivered when that same hand slipped between her thighs. She arched against his wide palm, filled suddenly with a sweet heat, a yearning.

It was dangerous to want a man so badly.

Finally, he raised his head, and the look in his eyes was smoldering. "I'll bet ol' Henry never kissed you like this," he said.

His words had to sift their way through a sensual fog to find her. Cody blinked back the tears that had gathered behind her eyes. Deacon could hate her for what she'd done to him, but Henry was innocent of any wrongdoing. "Please don't."

He tightened his grip on her. "Did he?"

"No." It sounded like a sob.

"Why did you throw it all away, Cody?" he demanded. "We could have been so good together." He gazed at her for a moment, as his hand pressed harder against the very heart of her desire. "It's better when you're older, you know. Think about it."

Finally he released her and stepped away, feeling the need to put some distance between them, both physically and emotionally. He was trembling from head to foot. He felt like hitting something, smashing his fist through a wall. He gazed at his surroundings, and he actually looked forward to all the work to be done, feeling the need to expend some of his anger and frustration and blatant arousal. Otherwise, he knew, he would end up saying or doing things he would only regret later. "Go inside, Cody," he said. "I'll carry all this out, then you can sort through it." Everything was crammed so tight, it was impossible to know what to trash or keep. "I need to be alone before I end up saying things I'll end up regretting later." Her eyes brimming with tears, Cody turned and fled.

Five

Two days later, Cody almost ran off the road when she spotted Deacon picking up trash on the side of the highway. At first she thought her eyes were playing tricks on her, then she recognized the black tank top he'd worn the day he'd helped her clean the garage. And even if she hadn't recognized the shirt, she would have recognized his jean-clad body. Nobody wore jeans that tight, and nobody looked that good in them. But what on earth was he doing out collecting trash, for heaven's sake!

Cody braked, pulled off the road, and put her car into reverse, backing down the grassy shoulder toward him. Once she'd gotten about ten yards away, she parked and turned off the engine. He glanced up nonchalantly as she stepped out of the car and closed the door.

"Deacon, what in the world!"

His eyes were hidden behind a pair of mirrored sunglasses; a red, sweat-soaked bandanna was tied around his forehead. "What are you doing here?" He didn't sound happy to see her.

"I had some errands to run." She glanced at the nail-tipped stick he clutched in one hand and the tall garbage bag in the other. "What are you doing?"

"That should be obvious, Cody," he said matter-of-factly. "I'm picking up trash."

"Who told you to do that?"

"My community service lady. You don't think I *volunteered* for this job, do you? Now, if you don't mind, I've got another couple of miles to clear before I call it a day. I figure by the time I've completed my hours, there won't be a piece of trash left in Calgary."

Cody was glad he was wearing the sunglasses, because she didn't want to have to look into his eyes at the moment. "Why, Deacon?" she asked softly. "Surely there are other jobs you can do. This—"

"Is losers' work?" he finished for her. "Is that what you were about to say?" He moved on, stabbing a crushed cigarette pack with his stick. Then he turned toward her and shoved his glasses high on his head. "And all this time I thought things couldn't get worse."

"I know Alma Black, Deacon. Your coordinator. She's a fair woman. I can't imagine her ordering you out here unless—" She paused.

"Unless I deserved it, right?" He didn't give her a chance to answer. "Well, there are worse jobs than picking up trash on the side of a highway. At least I can be alone here. I don't want a job where I have to put up with people staring and wondering and whispering behind my back. Besides, I don't like being around sick people."

"Sick people? What are you talking about?"

"Alma Black wanted me to work at the hospital."

"Doing what?"

"Providing entertainment and moral support for the sick and dying. I'm supposed to go into pediatrics and convince them, with my fun-guy personality, that everything is hunky-dory and they're all going to get better, even though some of them know damn good and well they aren't going to be around for their next birthday." He had to stop and catch his breath.

"What'd you tell Miss Black?"

"What do you think I told her?" he said, indicating his stick. "I said no."

"Did you tell her why?"

"You mean other than the fact that I'm not qualified?" He gave a snort. "I'm no child psychologist. I can't even deal with life these days, much less death, much less *cancer*! Those kids need someone who knows what he's doing. Hell, they need someone to come up with a cure."

"Did you tell Miss Black about your sister?" The look he gave her told her she was trespassing on a subject he didn't wish to discuss. But she knew if Alma Black was aware that Deacon's own sister had died at Calgary General after having lingered for weeks, the woman would not have asked him to take the job.

"No, I didn't tell Miss Black about Kimberly, and I don't *plan* to tell her. Now, can we drop this conversation?"

"Why won't you tell her?" she demanded.

He jabbed his stick in the ground angrily. "Because it's personal, okay?" he all but shouted.

"And because I'm sick and tired of having my life exposed to anyone who can afford the price of a tabloid. Nothing is sacred or private anymore. Those people enjoy splitting your guts open so the whole damn world can watch you bleed. Well, I've had it. They've already taken a year of my life. I want it back now."

"Miss Black wouldn't say anything, Deacon."

"Damn right she won't, because I'm not going to tell her. And neither are you."

"But Deacon—"

"No!" Cody jumped as he shouted the word into her face. "Look, I don't know how I've gone this long without the press finding out about Kimberly, but I'm thankful I still have something of my own, something I don't have to share with strangers. I don't want to have to relive my sister's illness and death through the tabloids."

She watched him work in silence for a moment. It was useless to argue. "Are you supposed to be working in the heat of the day like this, Deacon?" she asked, feeling the afternoon sun hot on her face.

He shook his head but didn't stop in his work. "I'm really supposed to do it in the morning, but I figure the longer I do it, the sooner I'll have my hours behind me. I've been at it three days now, so I'm really racking up the hours, aren't I?" The way he said it told her he thought it was going very slowly.

"Well—" She paused. "I guess I'd better go. Do you have plenty of water?"

"I'm fine, Cody. Just go, okay?" He sounded weary, but resigned to his decision.

Cody sensed he was embarrassed by the

labor he was being forced to perform. "Okay, Deacon, I'll go." She turned and made her way to her car.

Deacon's mood was low when he parked his car in Cody's garage at the end of the day. He felt so hot, he was certain the organs in his body had been cooked.

"Hi, Deacon."

He was vaguely aware of Katie standing at the mailbox as he made his way to the front of the house and up the steps to the porch. He mumbled something under his breath, then disappeared inside. Katie watched him go, her expression hurt that he didn't stop to chat.

". . . And I'm telling you, he didn't even seem to recognize me," Katie told her mother a few minutes later. "He just said something I didn't understand, then staggered up the steps."

Cody could tell that her daughter's feelings had been hurt. "You say he staggered?"

The girl nodded miserably, then paused as though wondering if maybe she had told her mother more than she'd wanted to. "Maybe he was just tired," she said after a moment.

Or drunk, Cody thought to herself, feeling her irritation flare at the thought of Deacon staggering up the steps in front of an impressionable twelve-year-old.

"And I probably get on his nerves. I mean, I'm always hanging around, and he's a big star and all. He doesn't have time to spend with some kid."

Cody listened and tried her best to keep her voice neutral when she spoke. "Why don't you go ahead and make a tossed salad to go with this great dinner you've planned for us," she suggested. "I'd like to have a word with Deacon."

"Oh, Mom, you're going to say something to him, aren't you?" Katie said. "Now he'll think I'm a rat."

"I won't even mention your name," Cody promised, "but if Deacon thinks he's going to start coming in drunk at the end of the day, he's got another think coming."

Cody pushed through the swinging door without another word. A minute later she found herself standing in front of Deacon's apartment. She knocked, and while she waited for him to answer, her anger mounted. How dare he do this to her, she thought. He'd probably stopped off at some seedy bar on the way home. And all afternoon she'd been feeling sorry for him and wishing she could call Alma Black in his defense. What a fool she was! Cody knocked again, this time louder, but there was no answer. Just who did he think he was? Well, she would ask him to leave, she told herself. She was not going to put up with the likes of Deacon Brody!

When Deacon still didn't answer, Cody was certain he was passed out cold, and the thought made her even angrier. She gritted her teeth and did what she had never done before. She turned the doorknob and pushed the door open.

He was on the sofa, facedown, one arm trailing to the floor. Cody stalked toward him, hands on hips, and gazed down at the man, thinking he was a sorry sight indeed. So this was the example he was trying to set for Katie! "Deacon Brody!" she said, her indignation flaring. "I *do* believe you'll have to find another place to live if you insist on staggering in like a wino off the streets in front of my daughter."

There was a grunt from the man. He opened his eyes, blinked at her, and spoke. "I can't . . . get up."

"Well, I should think not," she said, her voice rising sharply.

"I need a . . . drink."

Her anger flared. "Don't you think you've had enough for one day?"

He seemed to be having trouble focusing on her face and making sense of what she was saying. "I haven't had anything . . . like that."

"And you expect me to believe that? Why, you're soused!"

"The heat," he said. "It made me sick . . . to my stomach."

Cody snapped to attention. "The heat?" She studied his face and noted his ashen appearance. "You mean, you're not drunk?"

He closed his eyes. "Hardly."

Cody placed an open palm against his forehead. His skin was cold and clammy. "Oh Deacon, you *are* sick!" she said. "You must be suffering from heat exhaustion. Here, turn over on your back and let me help you." She went to work then, helping him roll onto his back, although he grumbled and complained that he wanted to be left alone. "Let's get this shirt off of you," she said, her fingers trembling as she tried to undo the buttons. He shrugged out of his top and fell limply to the sofa once more. The room seemed to shrink in size as his wide chest came into view. It was matted with the same black hair as he had on his head. Even in her state of distress, she couldn't help notice the taut muscles. He was rock-hard and solid as a concrete wall. Every inch a male. Next, she removed his shoes and socks, then propped his feet on a throw pillow. "I'm going to get you something to drink," she said, and hurried into the kitchen. He replied with a grunt.

When she returned, Cody held the back of his head up so he could sip his drink without spilling it. He made a face as soon as he tasted the liquid.

"Damn, what is this?" he said, shoving the glass away. "You trying to kill me?"

"It's salt water, Deacon. You *have* to drink it." He made a face that reminded her of Katie's when she was forced to take cough syrup for a cold. "This will make you better, Deacon. Otherwise, I'm going to have to take you to the emergency room."

His eyes met hers. "The hospital?"

Her gaze didn't waver. "Yes, the hospital."

"Okay, I'll drink."

Katie knocked on the door twenty minutes later and found Cody still ministering to the man. She peered around her mother to where Deacon was sprawled on the sofa. Although his color had improved, he still looked bad. "Is he drunk?" she whispered.

"No, he's *not* drunk," Deacon answered, drawing blushes from both mother and daughter.

Cody felt ashamed now for jumping to the wrong conclusion. "The heat got to him, honey. He's resting now. I was just about to come down."

"The lasagna is almost ready. Do you want me to bring him a plate?"

"I don't know. He probably doesn't much feel like eating."

"Excuse me, ladies," Deacon said from the couch. Their heads turned in his direction. "I'm well enough to answer for myself. Did someone mention lasagna? I can eat my weight in the stuff."

"Katie cooked dinner tonight as a home-economics project. I have to grade her on it. Would you like me to bring you a plate?"

"I'd rather join you," he said. "I get tired of eating all my meals alone."

"Do you think you're up to it?"

"I feel a lot better now."

Katie laughed. "Maybe we should make him sign something first, Mom. So he can't sue us if my lasagna makes him sick."

Deacon pondered it. "On second thought, maybe I'd better not." But he was clearly teasing Katie. He raised up slowly. "Would I have time to shower first? You really don't want me coming to dinner smelling like this, do you?"

They laughed. "We can wait," Cody told him, noting that he was looking better by the minute. "Take all the time you need." She finally left him when she was convinced he would be okay.

When Deacon knocked on Cody's door a half hour later, she was relieved to see, his color had returned. After a good night's sleep, he would be good as new. She let him in and led him into the dining room, where the table had been set with fancy place mats and cloth napkins. "Please sit down," she said, indicating one of the chairs. "Katie insists on doing everything by herself. So, how are you feeling? You look better."

He took the chair across from her. "The shower helped."

"Deacon, I owe you an apology," she said, wanting to get it over with before Katie joined them from the kitchen. "I said some things I shouldn't have."

He shrugged. "It's okay."

"No, it's not okay," she told him. "You were sick and needed help, and I let you down."

"You didn't let me down. I learned a long time ago not to count on people for anything. It's less frustrating that way, and you don't have to deal with a lot of disappointment." When he saw how his comment had hurt her, he was immediately remorseful. He covered her hand. "I'm sorry, Cody. I had no right to say that." He sighed. "I'm always saying the wrong things these days." He released her and raked one hand through his hair. "Not everybody has abandoned me," he said. "My family and my closest friends believe in me. *You* believe in me. I don't know why I have to be so hurtful at times."

"Maybe it's the only way you know how to get the hurt out," she said softly.

"That doesn't make it all right."

"No, it just makes it understandable."

He gazed at her for a moment. She had never looked prettier, not even at eighteen. Her hair was clean and healthy looking, and her complexion glowed as it had on their prom night. "Remember our first date?"

The question surprised her. Cody's mouth went completely dry. She sipped her water. "I met you at the Clover Grill, where you worked nights as a busboy." She smiled. "It was late; all the customers had gone. We were the only ones in the place. The owner had left you to close for him." She chuckled. "You said I could have anything I wanted."

He grinned. "And you let me down by ordering a tuna sandwich."

"It was the best tuna sandwich I'd ever had," she confessed.

He smiled. "It was the best date I'd ever had. Remember how we danced in front of the juke-box?"

"And you would only play slow songs?" she teased.

"That's because I wanted to hold you close. It was the only way I knew." He sighed and shook his head. He still wanted to hold her close, crush her in his arms. "I was a nervous wreck that night. Scared I'd do something wrong and you'd refuse to see me again."

She looked doubtful. "You, nervous?" she teased. "I'd never seen such a cool operator."

"It was all a front," he confessed with a grin. "To make you think I'd had a lot of experience."

"Didn't you?"

He shook his head. "You of all people should have realized I didn't have a lot of time for the opposite sex."

She knew he was referring to the fact that he'd had to work so much of the time.

"You were the prettiest girl in school, Cody Sherwood. Not to mention the most popular. I could never figure out what you saw in a bum like me."

"You were never a bum."

Deacon couldn't respond, because at that moment Katie carried in their salads. But there was a camaraderie between them that they hadn't felt in years. They were able to relax more with each other.

Katie waited breathlessly while Deacon took his first bite. Then, she asked nervously, "Well, what do you think? I know it's pretty hard to mess up lettuce and tomato, but I'm not very good at this."

"Excellent," he said, rolling his eyes in his head and making quite a production, despite the fact that his jaw muscles stung from the vinegary dressing.

Katie beamed. Once she'd served the garlic bread, she handed them both a piece of paper.

"Okay, you each have to fill out a questionnaire," she said. "Be truthful, though. Don't let the fact that I'm a great kid interfere with your decision." She turned for the door.

Deacon leaned closer to Cody once they were alone.

"What kind of salad dressing is this?"

"Italian. Homemade." She tried her best not to pucker as she ate it. "I think there's a tad too much vinegar, though. Katie sometimes gets carried away."

Which was proven true when they tasted the garlic bread. It had enough garlic on it for three loaves. Cody watched Deacon's reaction when he took a bite, and she thought she saw his eyes water. But he went to a lot of trouble to assure Katie he thought it was the best he'd ever tasted.

"There's a slight problem with the lasagna," Katie said, once she'd carried their empty salad bowls away. Her eyes darted frantically toward her mother. "Could I see you in the kitchen for a sec?"

"What is it, honey?" Cody asked when they were on the other side of the swinging door. She spotted the lasagna. "Oh, dear."

"I couldn't get the cheese to melt so I placed it under the broiler," Katie explained. "I burned the top to smithereens. Do you think Deacon will notice?"

Cody was tempted to tell the girl he would have to be blind and completely devoid of taste buds not to. "No, I think it'll be okay," she said instead. "Why don't we try to scrape some of the burnt part off?" She took a knife from the drawer.

Deacon didn't so much as crack a smile when Katie served the doctored lasagna a few minutes later. He waited until the girl had disappeared into the kitchen before saying anything. "What happened?"

Cody leaned close. "She burned the first three layers so badly, I had to rake them off. Just pretend you don't notice."

"Yeah, I can do that." He took a bite and coughed. Katie walked through the door and didn't miss it.

"I hope I didn't put too much oregano in it," she said. "When I started to sprinkle it into the egg mixture, the top came off, and I dumped almost the whole bottle in. I tried to spoon some of it out, though."

"It's wonderful," Cody told her daughter, looking proud. "Isn't it wonderful, Deacon?"

"Fabulous. She deserves an A plus."

"Ready for a second helping?" Katie asked Deacon. "Don't forget, you said you could eat your weight in it."

"Yes, I did say that, didn't I?"

"Be sure to save room for dessert," Katie warned. "I'm going to make strawberry short-cake." She glanced at her mother. "Do you think it's okay to take the strawberries out of the freezer to thaw now?"

Once dinner was behind them, Katie insisted Cody and Deacon retire to the front porch while she cleaned the kitchen and made coffee. "Let me help you," Cody told the girl. Having seen the kitchen, she knew it would take Katie forever to get things put away. Not only that, she didn't want to be alone on the front porch with Deacon.

"No, Mom, I have to do it by myself," the girl insisted. "It's part of my grade. Besides, it's the least I can do after I ruined dessert."

"You didn't *ruin* dessert," Cody told her. "We still enjoyed the cake and whipped cream." But she knew the girl wasn't convinced. When Cody had told her to stick the frozen strawberries in the microwave for a few minutes to thaw, Katie had obviously hit the wrong buttons. By the time she'd thought to check on the berries, they had all but disintegrated. Cody knew it would take a week to clean the inside of the microwave.

She and Deacon exchanged amused glances and allowed themselves to be relocated to the porch. Deacon waited until they were alone before he said anything. "I hope they're teaching her to do more than cook in that class," he said. "I'm not sure it's a talent she's going to be able to fall back on."

Cody giggled. "You think dinner was bad, you should see the dress she made last fall. Luckily, her teacher is trying to teach the girls a little bit of everything. Last semester they had to memorize everything beneath the hood of the car. I

haven't decided where the child is more dangerous, in a garage or in the kitchen."

"Too bad she doesn't see her father more
often," he said. "My dad was the one who taught
me how to take care of a car."

Cody shifted uncomfortably in her chair. It
was not a subject she cared to pursue. "It just
hasn't been convenient for the two of them to be
together often."

"Convenient for whom?" he asked.

"Everyone concerned," she said, being delib-
erately vague.

"Your ex-husband doesn't sound like anybody I'd care to meet."

"How can you say that about him?" she said
sharply. "You don't even know him."

"I don't have to know him to know that a
father should spend time with his child," Deacon said matter-of-factly. "I don't care if the two
of you *are* divorced, that shouldn't make a
difference where Katie is concerned."

"Katie was only four years old when Henry
and I split up. And he does try to see her when
he can."

"'When he can'? Durham isn't that far away,
Cody."

"He calls," she pointed out. "And Katie calls
him whenever she wants to."

"And you think that's enough? The girl needs
her father, Cody."

She was weary of people telling her how bad
off Katie was without her father. They had
managed perfectly well on their own. Not only
that, Katie seemed happy and well adjusted for
the most part. True, the girl got out of hand
once in a while, but she didn't do anything
serious or out of the ordinary for someone her

age. Nothing Cody couldn't handle. Besides, it wasn't as though they were the only single-parent family in Calgary.

"Katie has me," she said after a moment. "That's all she needs."

Deacon looked at her. "You don't really believe that, do you?"

She was more than a little irritated at the remark. "Of course I do. It's not as if she hasn't had any male influence. My father spent a lot of time with her before he died."

"That's not the same."

"Look, Deacon, I really don't need your advice on how to raise my daughter," she said tightly. "I think I've done a pretty good job with Katie." She stood and crossed the porch. "Anyway, what do *you* know about children? You're hardly in a position to criticize me."

He watched her from his chair. "You mean 'cause I've screwed up my own life so badly?"

"Not at all."

He unfolded himself slowly and stood. "Why don't you say it? I have a reputation as a hell-raiser, and now I have a police record. I've no right telling you how to raise your daughter."

"You simply don't have any experience with children. You couldn't possibly know what it's like. I've done my best with Katie, and I'm tired of people criticizing me or suggesting otherwise."

He looked surprised. "Who says you haven't done a good job? I never meant to imply that."

"My parents, when they were alive. They thought I should be more strict with her. And what about Sheriff Busby? He thinks I should take a hickory stick, as he calls it, to her."

"What does he know?"

Cody went on as though she hadn't heard him. "I don't want Katie to perform like one of those dolls where you pull a string and she says all the right words. I don't want her raised the way I was, Miss Prim-and-Proper without a thought of her own. All my life I've tried to please people . . . do the right thing. It got me nowhere."

He was quiet for a moment. "Is that why you dumped me, Cody? To please your parents? Were you trying to do the *right* thing?"

She was so tired of trying to answer that question for him. "We were only eighteen, Deacon. I wanted to be on my own for a while. I wanted an education. And you wanted to go to Nashville. So yes, I was trying to do the right thing."

"Are you happy now, Cody?"

He was waiting for her to tell him how badly she'd messed up, to confess that she never *would* be happy without him. But she would not give him the satisfaction of telling him she wanted to be a part of his life, because she knew there was no place in it for her now. "Yes, I'm happy, Deacon. Katie has made all the difference."

He pondered it. "I guess that's all you can ask for, then."

"What do you mean?"

He gazed out at the stars, wondering how she had managed to convince herself she was better off without him. It hurt to know that she could dismiss him so easily. It angered him that she had not lived to regret giving him up. "Well, you obviously have everything you need," he said. "I'm happy for you," he added, studying her in the moonlight. But the look on his face said otherwise.

Cody was aware that he was staring at her. "Yes, I have all I need," she answered. But in her heart she knew she was only fooling herself and him. Thankfully, they were prevented from discussing it further when Katie stepped out onto the porch with their coffee.

Six

The following day, Cody opened her front door and found Maybelline Carter standing there with her fat hands folded together in front of her like small hams, an imitation alligator purse hanging from one arm.

"Maybelline, what a surprise. Won't you come in?"

The woman hesitated. Her face was splotchy from the afternoon heat, her nostrils pinched as though she smelled something bad. "For a moment, I suppose." She stepped inside and waited for Cody to close the door. Even though she looked somewhat relieved to find it cool inside, her stance remained rigid and unyielding.

"Please sit down," Cody told her, indicating a chair. She caught the scent of medicated face cream and a gardenia-scented perfume that reminded her of the elderly ladies at church who wore flowery dresses and old-fashioned pillbox hats.

"I'll stand," Maybelline said. "This won't take long. It concerns my niece and your daughter."

"Oh? Is something wrong?" She couldn't imagine why the woman was there. Unless she wanted to start trouble, of course. But what did Katie have to do with it?

Maybelline didn't waste any time. "Ann-Marie had to stay after school last week. Again," she added. "For acting up in the library with Katie. The second time this month. A couple of weeks ago the two were hauled into the office for passing notes."

"I didn't know."

"Of course you didn't. Which is why I'm here. My sister, Mary, thought it was time we brought it to your attention."

Once again Cody found herself on the defensive where her daughter was concerned. Was Maybelline insinuating that she thought Cody was too busy with other things to know what was going on with her own child? "Why didn't Mary come to me with this?" she asked. "She and I have been able to talk in the past."

"That should be obvious, Cody. Mary doesn't feel comfortable in your home with that . . . that man here." She angled a glance at the ceiling. "Nor does she feel comfortable with Ann-Marie spending time here anymore. I suppose you thought all that out, though, before you decided to bring *him* under your roof."

It didn't take a genius to figure out who the woman was referring to. "What are you trying to say, Maybelline? That you don't want Ann-Marie and Katie to be friends anymore? You realize they've been best friends since first grade."

"Perhaps you should have considered that before you allowed a known sex offender to move in. You don't think I'd allow my niece to spend the night here anymore." When Cody didn't answer, she went on. "Besides, those two are more worried about their social life than their grades these days. It's time to put a stop to it."

Cody didn't quite know what to say. It was bad enough that people were canceling on her and creating more of a financial strain. She had known all along that Maybelline Carter was behind it, but she had thought the woman would tire of it soon and give up. Now it seemed as if nothing would stop her. And now it was worse, because it affected Katie. Nobody was going to hurt her daughter and get away with it.

Cody's temper flared at the thought of *anyone* injuring her little girl. "Maybelline Carter, you are the most vicious woman I've ever met," she said after a moment. "Haven't you got anything better to do with your time than create problems for other people? No wonder you never married."

Maybelline let out a loud gasp and drew her handbag close as though to protect herself from the accusations. "Well, I never!"

"That's right, Maybelline," Cody said as she opened the door. "And you probably never will. Now, get out of here before I lose my temper and forget I'm a lady."

The heavyset woman hitched her head high and marched out in a huff. Cody slammed the door so hard the house shook. When she turned around she found Katie standing in the doorway.

"I heard everything," the girl said. "That woman isn't happy unless she's stirring up trouble."

"I think she feels it's her duty," Cody said.

"She's trying to put you out of business, too, isn't she? That's why we've been getting all those cancellations." Katie stepped closer. "What are we going to do?"

"I'll think of something."

Katie looked as though she might cry. "Why does she have to do this, Mom? Why does she have to be so hateful? Why would she want to destroy my friendship with Ann-Marie?"

Cody put her arms around her daughter. She was tempted to follow Maybelline out to her car and give her another piece of her mind. When somebody hurt her, she simply got angry; when Katie got hurt, she became a crazy lady. "Some people are so miserable they don't want to see other people enjoy life. We'll work it out, honey. I promise."

Katie nodded. "I'm going for a walk," she said.

"Want some company?"

The girl shook her head. "Naw, I just want to be alone for a while."

Katie was more than a mile from the house when Deacon, on his way home, spotted her and pulled his car to the side of the road. He pressed a button, and the window slid down silently. "Need a ride?" he called out. He knew something was bothering the girl the moment he caught sight of her expression. But he knew better than to ask. He sensed Katie was a lot like himself in that respect. She wouldn't talk about her troubles until she darn well felt like it.

Katie looked happy to see him. She leaned into the window. "I've never been in a Lotus before."

"First time for everything. Hop in."

She opened the door and climbed in. "Oh, wow!" she said, noting the hand-stitched leather seats. "What a cool car. What can it do?"

"Zero to sixty in four-point-seven. I don't suppose you'd want to drive it?"

Katie's eyes looked as though they might pop right out of her head and roll onto the luxurious dashboard. "Me?" she said, her voice little more than a squeak.

"Unless your mother is expecting you home right away," he said. She shook her head. "We'll take it someplace where there's not a lot of traffic." He paused, his look stern. "I can teach you if you like."

Katie didn't hesitate. "Of course I wanna learn. Think I can do it?"

"Sure, where's a good place?"

"Out near where they're building the new high school. The parking lot is huge. There's not much traffic this time of day and, besides, maybe somebody'll recognize me. A high school guy."

He tried to affect a menacing look, but he knew it was lost on the girl. "I catch you chasin' after high school guys, and I'm going to turn you over my knee, Katie darlin'. Stop trying to grow up so fast."

Katie ducked her head and offered him a demure look. "Yes sir. I promise I won't look at a high school boy till I'm in my thirties."

He winked. "Good girl. I'd hate to have to lock you up in a convent for the rest of your life." He smiled. At the same time, he wondered why he was so protective of her. Because she was Cody's daughter, he told himself. Because her real father didn't seem to have much of an interest. And because he couldn't stand the thought of her getting hurt.

The soon-to-be Calgary Senior High was less than five miles away, located on a stretch of road that was only used by the high school crowd for cruising. On the way, Deacon ran through the gears for Katie. "Think you can handle it?" he asked, once he'd parked and she'd gotten behind the wheel and fastened her seat belt.

"Nothin' to it," she said, shoving the gear into first. She stepped on the accelerator, and the car shot forward like a small rocket. "Jeeze Louise!" she cried. "Lookit this thing go!"

Deacon placed a hand against the dashboard. "Whoa there, girl!" he said. "Let's make sure you know what you're doing before you try to break the sound barrier."

Katie slowed considerably. "Wow, this thing really burns rubber." She glanced at Deacon. "How do I look?"

He smiled, thinking again how much she resembled Cody. He wondered if there was any resemblance to her father. "You look great," he said. "You look like you were born to drive a Lotus, Katie darlin'." She beamed with pleasure.

Katie drove around the parking lot for the next fifteen or twenty minutes, honking her horn once or twice.

"Ohmygod, do you see who's pulling in here?" Katie asked.

Deacon took a closer look at the old Buick turning into the lot. It looked as though it were being held together by rust and mud. The back window seemed to vibrate from the music inside, and he couldn't help but wonder if the boys riding in it were all deaf. "Who is it?" he asked.

"It's Robbie Carson and his younger brother, Billy."

"No kidding." Deacon tried to sound impressed. "Who is Robbie Carson and his younger brother, Billy?"

"Billy plays junior varsity football at Calgary Middle School."

"Oh, *that* Billy Carson. Why didn't you say so?" It was obvious he was teasing her.

"Ohmygod, they see me!" she cried. "Now what am I going to do?"

Deacon could tell the group of boys were both surprised and impressed. "Just hold your head up high and pretend it's nothing out of the ordinary for you to be driving a hundred-thousand-dollar car, darlin'."

"Ohmygod!"

Deacon glanced at her. "*Now* what?"

"Look who's behind them."

"What, another football jock?" Deacon glanced around quickly, then sighed when he recognized Sheriff Busby's patrol car and the flashing blue light on top.

Cody was pacing the floor when Katie and Deacon pulled into the front yard twenty minutes later. She all but raced down the front steps to the car. "Are you okay?" she asked her daughter the minute she climbed out.

"Sure, Mom. Deacon and I were just—"

"I know what you and Deacon were doing, young lady, and I don't approve for one minute." She crossed her arms and tapped her foot, giving

Deacon a look of sheer disapproval. "Sheriff Busby just called me."

Deacon exchanged glances with Katie. "Look, Cody, I can explain," he began.

"Oh, really?" she said in a saccharine-sweet voice. "I'm going to enjoy hearing this."

"We were just having a little fun, Cody, that's all."

"Fun? Fun? You call breaking the law '*fun*'?"

"It's not like we robbed a bank or something. I just thought Katie would enjoy driving the Lotus."

"With no driver's license," Cody pointed out. She glared at her daughter. Her stomach was still tied in knots from Sheriff Busby's call. She had imagined all sorts of horrors, most of them involving Katie and Deacon lying lifeless and mangled among the twisted metal of his car. "I want to know who you think you are for just whisking my daughter off like that in the first place. Can you imagine how I felt when folks started calling, saying they saw the two of you heading toward the new high school site? Can you *imagine*?" Once again, she'd felt like a negligent mother for not being able to put a finger on her daughter, for not knowing her whereabouts. Then she'd learned Katie was with Deacon and she'd become even more anxious. But not because of his reputation.

Deacon's eyes were full of anger. "So that's it," he said. "You're not really upset about your daughter driving without a license, you're more concerned that people will think something else is going on." When Cody opened her mouth to object, he cut her off. "You're a hypocrite, Cody."

"What is *that* supposed to mean?"

"Meaning you can tell me all you want about

how you know I'm innocent of the crime I was charged with, but when it comes right down to it, you don't believe in me any more than the rest of them."

"That's not true!"

"Isn't it? Well, rest assured I didn't lay a hand on the girl," he all but growled. "I just wanted to spend a little time with her. Believe me, it won't happen again." He slammed out the door a moment later.

When Cody turned to her daughter, she found tears rolling down the girl's cheeks. "Thanks a lot, Mom. First I lose my best friend, and now Deacon doesn't want to have anything to do with me." She fled from the room without another word.

It was almost eleven o'clock when Cody knocked on the door to Deacon's apartment. After having sulked all evening, Katie had finally gone to bed early and was snoring gently when Cody checked on her at ten. Standing in front of Deacon's door and waiting for him to answer, Cody wiped her damp hands on her shorts and took a deep breath. She spoke the minute he opened the door.

"Can we talk?"

"Why, did you think up some new names to call me?"

"I came to apologize."

He opened the door and stepped aside so she could come in. "Have a seat." He motioned toward the sofa, waited until she sat down, then took the chair across from her.

Cody thought he looked nothing like a country-western star who'd traveled all over the world and sung for millions. Still, he was about as handsome as they came, wearing simple cutoffs and a comfortable T-shirt. There was something about the man that set him apart and made him larger than life, something other than just good looks. "I feel like a heel," she confessed. "Not for getting upset about Katie driving your car, mind you, but for letting what other people think matter so much. It's a hard habit to break when you've done it for twelve years. But I want you to know, I wasn't worried you'd harm Katie in any way." She went on when he continued to look doubtful. "You have to believe that, Deacon."

"So you were more concerned what people might think if they saw Katie and me together. I'm not sure which is worse, Cody."

"She's my daughter, and I want to protect her. That includes protecting her from idle gossip as well. You can't fault me for that, Deacon." She paused and sighed. "When you're a single parent, people are forever criticizing you, they're always careful to show you where you're going wrong with your child. I suppose I'm a little defensive about it, because every time I make the slightest mistake with Katie, I feel like an absolute failure, and I can't deal with feeling that way." She paused. "I sometimes feel as if I've failed in every relationship I've ever tried to develop."

"People would criticize you if you had a husband," he said. "That's just the way they are. It's human nature."

She pondered it. "I've always tried to be everything to Katie," she said. "Her mother, her friend, her confidante. I've read every book written on the subject of parenting, but I can't seem to perfect this thing called motherhood." She smiled ruefully. "It's like when a couple of people called me tonight and asked if I knew Katie was joyriding in your car. Well, I thought I must be some kind of awful mother not to know exactly where my daughter was and what she was doing. That sort of thing really gets to me, I'm afraid."

He became thoughtful. "You can't possibly know where Katie is every minute of the day, Cody. You're going to have to trust her to make the right decisions. And then you're going to have to be there for her when she doesn't."

"It's hard to let go." She felt the sting of tears. "Katie is all I have. I want to walk in front of her and smooth the path so she doesn't stumble or get scratched by thorns along the way."

He was touched to the core by her tears. He reached out and took one of her hands and raised it to his lips. "We all stumble, Cody. That's life. The object is to learn how to pick ourselves up, dust off our backsides, and go on."

Her voice trembled when she spoke. "Is that what you're doing now?"

He offered her a grim look.

"Yeah, I reckon I am." He squeezed her hand. She had never looked sweeter than she did then, with her eyes glimmering like jewels. Finally, one lone tear slid silently down her cheek. "Come here," he said, giving her hand a tug. Cody hesitated, then stood and gazed down at him with uncertainty. He reached for her and pulled her onto his lap. "Don't cry, baby," he said, gathering her against him. He held her for a moment, feeling his heart in his throat. She was soft and sweet smelling, and every emotion in his body stirred, emotions he'd thought long since dead, emotions that were both frightening and wonderful. Then, because he could stand it no longer, he lowered his head and captured her lips with his.

The kiss was gentle and unhurried. Cody slipped her arms around Deacon's neck and clung to him as he raised his lips slightly, then gathered the salty tears near the corners of her mouth with his tongue before kissing her once more. They embraced, they cuddled. The moment was loving and nurturing, each of them giving as much as receiving. Cody inhaled his scent and opened her mouth wide to accompany his eager tongue. He tasted wonderful. She was reminded of the first kiss they'd shared. Suddenly, she couldn't get enough of him. Her own tongue explored the warm, dark corners of his mouth, and she knew she would never find a more delicious man. They paused every so often and gazed into each other's eyes as though wanting to make sure it was real, as though half afraid it was just an illusion.

Deacon stood and lifted her in his arms, and Cody nuzzled her face against his neck, seeking his warmth and the clean scent of him. She was vaguely aware of being carried from the room, and the next thing she knew, she was being lowered onto something soft. His bed. She sighed and drew him close.

Clothes became a hindrance, but one that could be overcome. Deacon undressed her slowly, kissing each spot he bared as though he'd just unwrapped something precious and rare. Deacon kissed and tasted. He started with her fingers, pressing his lips against each tip, then sweeping his tongue between them. He kissed her palms, her wrist, the length of her arm, then pressed his mouth against the inside of her elbow, where her pulse beat a frantic message against his lips. He cupped her breasts, and she was certain she'd found paradise.

A sigh rose from her lips like a sweet song when Deacon finally closed his mouth around one nipple. The gentle, tugging motion stirred something low in her belly. Her own hands never stilled. They explored the hard lines of his body, taking pleasure in the tight, corded muscles along his back and shoulders, the coarse hair on his chest, the downy fuzz that covered the back of his neck.

Deacon made love to her navel, swirling his tongue around it, then dipping inside. Cody arched against him as he moved his lips to her thighs. His mouth was hot. Heat met heat. The ache in her belly was as sweet as it was unbearable. She opened herself more fully, and gave in to each heady sensation. Inside, she felt her heart swell with emotion, and she was almost moved to tears by the sweetness and the tenderness Deacon's touch evoked. This is the way it had always been for them, this meeting of hearts and souls. And she had walked away from it all.

Finally, Deacon entered her, and she was caught up in something so powerful, it took her breath away. Cody could only hang on for dear life and pray that she would still be sane when she reached the other side.

Deacon grunted and muttered something incoherent.

Cody's ears roared.

They shuddered in each other's arms.

It was a long time before either of them spoke. They simply lay there, bodies damp and spent, but jubilant. Deacon watched her, the peaceful look on her face, the way her lashes fell crescentlike across her closed eyes.

"Cody?"

"Hmm?"

"I still love you."

She opened her eyes and gazed back at him, and when she spoke her voice trembled. "I never stopped loving you."

The knowledge filled him with something good, warmed the dark places in his heart, took some of the sting out of the bitterness that had been such a big part of him for the past year. He felt hopeful for the first time in months. "We need to talk," he said after a moment. When she nodded, he went on. "I want to know about Henry Cox."

Cody raised the coffee cup to her lips and took a sip. It was strong and black and just what she needed at the moment to calm the butterflies in her stomach. Leaning against the counter wearing only his cutoffs, Deacon sipped as well. He watched her from over the rim of his coffee cup.

"Well?" he said.

Cody had asked him to make the coffee so she could have time to sort through the things he wanted to know. She was still nervous, though, and it showed. Finally, she set her cup down and took a deep breath.

"I don't know what I can tell you except that I met Henry at a time when I really needed a friend." She glanced up at Deacon. His face was completely devoid of emotion. "I was devastated after our breakup," she said. "My parents drove me to Durham a couple of days later, and I stayed with Mr. and Mrs. Cox until school started. Henry, their oldest son, had been attending Duke for a couple of years, and he sort of took me under his wing." She glanced at Deacon. His jaw was unyielding, granitelike. "We became good friends."

"Obviously."

His tone of voice hurt. She had to make him understand. But how could he? "His parents treated me like a daughter." She paused. "Anyway, we got married within a couple of months."

"Did you love him?"

Her voice shook. "Yes. He was good to me."

"Then why'd you divorce?"

"I suppose we grew apart."

"Have you stayed in touch with him?"

"He visits at Christmas. He sends me flowers on my birthday. We're still friends, if that's what you want to know, and he calls Katie often. There's no hard feelings between us. And his parents always make a point to stop by whenever they come through."

"How nice."

She didn't miss the sarcasm in his voice. "Why do you say that?"

"Because no matter how hard you try to sugarcoat the whole thing, Cody, it's still not right. Your daughter is still running around without a father to guide her—"

"Oh, so we're going to fight about that again," she said dully.

"No, we're not going to fight. But I want you to

know how I feel about the whole thing." He sighed and raked his hand through his hair. "Look, it's hard for me to think of you with another man, but I'll get over it. I wasn't living in a monastery all those years myself. Somehow, we'll have to put it behind us. But I love you, and I'd like to give us a second chance."

She glanced up at him. "What does that mean exactly?"

"I'm not sure. I'd like to take it one day at a time, if you don't mind. Everything is happening so fast. I need time to deal with my own problems first. I don't want to drag you and Katie down with me."

She wanted to tell him it was okay, that she would go anywhere with him now. But she didn't. There were too many uncertainties at the moment, too many things that needed to be resolved. Such as what he would do when he'd served his sentence in Calgary. She couldn't imagine living in Memphis with Katie while he toured three hundred days out of the year. Katie. That was something else she was going to have to deal with, and she didn't look forward to it one bit.

When Cody looked up, she found Deacon standing over her. He held out his hands, and she placed hers in them. He pulled her up. "Cody, I think we can make it this time, if we give it half a chance. What d'you say? You want to try again?"

She was scared, but she smiled bravely and nodded. "Yes." She only hoped they could work out their problems.

"This time I want complete honesty between us," Deacon continued. "No holding back. It's going to be tough enough getting through the

next few months. I have to know where I stand
with you at all times."

"Deacon?" There were still doubts and unfin-
ished business. He'd said he wanted honesty.

"Just say yes, Cody."

"Yes."

Seven

When Deacon arrived home the following afternoon and locked his car away, he found Katie sitting on the porch, looking for all the world as though she'd just lost her best friend. "Why so glum?" he asked, coming to a halt on the top step.

Katie didn't look up. "I'm grounded."

"Because of yesterday?" She nodded. "For how long?"

"Two weeks."

Deacon sighed and took one of the wicker chairs near her. "I'm sorry. It's my fault. I'll see what I can do."

"I wouldn't talk to her right now. She's madder than a hornet."

He arched one brow. He'd been looking forward to seeing Cody all day. The last time he'd laid eyes on her, she'd been wearing a wide grin. Of course, they'd just made wild, passionate love at the time. Although he'd wanted to stop by and see her that morning, he figured she'd be tied up getting Katie off to school. "Why's she mad?"

"We had another cancellation." When he looked confused, she went on. "You know, Mother gives parties and meetings and stuff. Well, three people have called to cancel." For a moment, Katie looked as though she might cry. "It's that old biddy Maybelline Carter causing trouble again," she said. "She's trying to ruin my party too."

Maybelline Carter. The name rang a definite bell. He had spent so much time in her office for being tardy that he could remember what color her walls were painted. Maybelline had considered him lazy and good-for-nothing. It never occurred to her that he overslept most mornings because he'd had to work till after midnight the night before. But why was Maybelline giving Cody a hard time? "Slow down, Katie, you lost me. Now, take a deep breath and tell me what's really going on."

When Deacon entered the kitchen, he found Cody slamming pots and pans and cabinet doors. She glanced up in surprise at the sight of him. "Oh, Deacon, hi. I was just cleaning the kitchen."

"It sounded more like you were trying to take it apart," he told her.

She offered him a derisive smile. "Yes, well, it's been one of those kinds of days."

He closed the distance between them and took her in his arms, planting a firm kiss on her lips. "I missed you."

She could only nod and give in to the pleasure

of being held by him. "I missed you too." She had thought of little else all day. In fact, she had spent a lot of time daydreaming about the night before. They had made love once more after their talk in the kitchen, then she'd slipped downstairs quietly, praying Ms. Vickers would not hear her leave. There had been a lot to smile about all day, even with the nagging doubts that plagued her from time to time, even though she knew they would have to come to terms with their past before it was over, before they could begin to discuss their future. Then she'd gotten another cancellation that afternoon, and her mood had soured dramatically.

"I smell like a wet billy goat," he said laughingly. "I haven't showered yet."

He could have smelled like manure for all she cared. She liked being close to him. "Want something cold to drink first?" He nodded, and they moved apart slowly, reluctantly. Deacon took a seat at the table while she put ice in a glass and filled it with tea. She joined him at the table, and he sipped in silence for a moment.

Finally, he put the glass down and regarded her. "I hear you grounded Katie."

"That's right."

"It was my fault. I instigated the whole thing."

She nodded. "Yes, but you're a grown man, and I have no control over what you do. I like to think I still have some where my daughter is concerned." She paused. "Besides, Katie has a mind of her own. She should have used better judgment."

"What if Katie and I share the blame here?" he suggested.

She looked amused. "Okay, you're grounded to your apartment for two weeks."

He chuckled. "You'll visit me, won't you?"

"See, you're just like Katie. Already trying to get extra privileges."

He took her hand. "Look, Cody, I don't want to see the girl punished for something I caused. I don't know anything about kids, but when I saw her looking all wrung out yesterday, I just wanted to cheer her up. I wish you wouldn't be so hard on her."

"Boy, you're good."

He grinned and squeezed her hand. "Thank you."

She pulled her hand away. This was her daughter they were discussing, and she needed her wits about her. "I'll think about it," she said. "But I'm not making any promises. Is there anything else?"

He drained his glass and set it down. "Yeah, I want to talk about these cancellations you're having."

"I see you've been talking to my daughter, the informant."

"I have ways of getting facts out of people. She's still wearing the bamboo stalks I shoved under her fingernails."

"Katie couldn't keep a secret if someone offered her a private telephone and a Saks credit card."

"So what's this all about? You've had three cancellations in less than a week?"

"It happens sometimes."

"Are you trying to say it has nothing to do with me living here? Come on, Cody, do I have 'stupid' written all over my face?"

She waved the remark aside. "It'll all blow over soon."

"Before or after they run you out of business?"

She didn't want to tell him how close to the truth he was. "I'll survive," she said. "It's not the first time I've had business problems. It's a chance you take when you go out on your own."

"Let me help you, Cody."

"No."

"Dammit, why do you have to be so stubborn?" He slammed his fist against the table. "I love you. I want to help. I can afford it. Besides, this is all my fault."

Cody stood and crossed the room to the sink. "I want to do this on my own, Deacon."

He stood and walked over to her, slipping his arms around her waist from behind. "When did you get to be such an independent little cuss?" he asked, nuzzling his face against the back of her neck.

She shivered. She could feel his arousal pressing against her soft hips. "I just like knowing I can provide for myself and my daughter," she said with a great deal of difficulty.

He turned her around and gazed into her eyes, thinking she had never looked more beautiful or desirable. He wanted to make love to her as he had the night before. He wanted to lose himself in her softness, forget his troubles. Only Cody had the power to do that to him. "Don't forget, you gave me a place to live when nobody else wanted to rent to me. I owe you. If things get too tough for you, I want to know. Deal?" She nodded, and he kissed her. When he raised his head, he was smiling. "Do you plan to come up later?"

She would've had to be a complete imbecile to miss his meaning. "I don't know. It depends on what time Katie falls asleep tonight." He could accuse her of being a hypocrite again if he wanted, but she didn't care. She didn't want Katie to know about them just yet. Not until she knew herself where their relationship was going.

"I could always chase her around the block in my car a few dozen times," he offered with a grin. "That ought to wear her down."

Cody laughed and slapped him playfully. "You're terrible!"

He hauled her against his solid body. "Yeah, I am, aren't I? But I think that's one of the things you like best about me."

The following morning, Alma Black ushered Deacon into her office and indicated an empty chair. "This is a surprise, Mr. Brody," she said. "I wasn't expecting to see you until next week. How's the cleanup going on Highway 46?"

His look was somber. "You were right, Miss Black. I've learned my lesson, and I'm ready to cooperate now." He paused. "I'm just sorry I gave you such a hard time in the beginning." When she didn't so much as bat an eye, he continued. "Anyway, I have an idea how I can best serve this town and make you guys look so good, they'll give you the budget increase you've been asking for." He saw that he'd caused her to raise an eyebrow by mentioning budgeting problems. He'd been acting on a whim, of course, because he had no way of knowing about the finances regarding her agency. But he also knew there wasn't a federally or state-funded organization in existence that didn't have budget problems. "Well, what d'you say?" he asked.

She regarded him. "You're very good, Mr. Brody. What did you have in mind?"

Deacon waited until he had their full, undivided attention. "Katie, stop fidgeting; this'll only take a minute."

Cody gave an exasperated sigh. "Deacon, would you just tell us what this is all about?" she said.

The three of them were sitting at the kitchen table sipping iced tea, having gathered there when Deacon had announced he had something very important to discuss with them. He'd even given Cody a pad so she could take notes.

"Our hospital is too small," he said.

Cody and her daughter exchanged looks. "That's what you wanted to talk to us about?" Cody asked.

"I want to build a center for cancer patients," he said, "with an emphasis on treating children."

Cody met his gaze. His look was unwavering. "When did you decide this?"

"I think I've always known it was something I needed to do. I just didn't have the courage until now."

"I think that's a great idea, Deacon," Katie told him. "Don't you, Mom?"

Cody smiled at her daughter. "You'd go along with anything he said at the moment," she teased, "since I knocked a week off your restriction." Katie tossed Deacon one of her hero-worship looks, and he winked in response. "So what's your plan, Deacon?" Cody asked.

"First I get my business manager to call a press conference," he said, "and announce the idea. I figure we can get a couple of hundred people to come, at a thousand bucks a head."

Katie's eyes almost popped out of her skull. "A thousand bucks!"

"That's chicken feed to these people."

Cody was frowning. "Deacon, you said 'we.' What have I got to do with this?"

"I want you to give the party here."

She almost turned over her iced tea. "No way. No-sir-ee!"

"I'll hire as many people as you need to help you. I'll rent tables and chairs and whatever else you need."

"No!"

"Mom, say yes!" Katie cried.

"It'll be the mother of all charity events," he told them.

"Deacon, have you gone and lost your poor mind?" Cody asked. "First of all, how are you going to get these people here? There's no airport."

"We have a small airport. Most of them will come in private planes. I'll arrange for a limousine service for those who fly into Winston-Salem."

"And where will these people stay? Have you forgotten we have no *nice* hotel in Calgary?"

"We'll ask the townspeople to open their homes to them."

Cody shook her head. "This whole thing

sounds crazy," she said. "How do you think the people of Calgary are going to feel knowing they can't afford to come to your party, especially since they feel you've snubbed them once already?"

"They won't have to pay to attend as long as they agree to play host or hostess to our guests."

"When exactly do you plan to hold this event?"

"One month from tonight."

"One month! You *are* crazy!"

"We'll need to start making a list of those we want to invite right away, so I can have invitations printed. Start writing, Cody. We don't have any time to lose."

"I have to call somebody first," Katie said, almost toppling her chair as she jumped up and raced out of the room. Cody still hadn't made a move to pick up the pencil Deacon had given her.

"What's wrong?" he said.

"Deacon, do you realize the kinds of questions you're going to be asked at a press conference?"

His smile faded slightly. "Yeah, I've been thinking about it all day. I'm sure my attorney will want to brief me first." He took her hand and squeezed it. "I can handle it, Cody."

"What about your sister? Word is bound to leak out once the reporters start snooping around asking questions. And you know they will."

"I'm going to save them the trouble," he said. "I'll tell them everything they want to know so they don't *have* to dig." He grinned. "Of course, they'll want to know the names of any old flames I had before I made it big. I hope you don't mind if I give them yours." He winked. "So if you've got any skeletons in your closet, I'd suggest you bring them out now."

Cody froze in her seat and felt something cold close its fist around her heart. They were going to question *her*? "Uh, Deacon?"

"Start writing, Cody," he said. "We have to move fast now."

Eight

Alma Black leafed through the notebook containing the notes Deacon and Cody had made concerning the party. "This is a pretty impressive guest list. You think they'll come?"

Deacon nodded. "Yeah, they'll come. When you got as much money as some of these people, you have to attend your fair share of charity events so you don't feel guilty about having more than everybody else."

"Do you feel guilty for having money, Mr. Brody?"

He pondered it. "I'd feel bad if I'd inherited it for doing nothing. But I work hard for my money."

She nodded after a moment and handed him his list. "I'm pleased you've decided to do something for this town, Mr. Brody, but this isn't likely to eat up all your community service hours, now is it?"

He looked surprised. "What do you mean?"

"I have a job for you."

"Aw, hell, lady. Don't you ever let up?"

"No, it's my job to make your life miserable." She smiled as she said it. It was the first time Deacon could remember her doing anything more than frowning at him. "There's a small shelter in town for homeless men. The man running it has been hospitalized and will be off his feet for a few weeks. I'd like you to take over in his absence."

"Why me?"

"Because you know what it's like to have nothing, and you know what it takes to become successful. Some of these men have drug and alcohol problems, and a couple of them have just had too much bad luck."

"Look, I'm not a social worker. What do I know about this sort of thing?"

"You don't need a degree in psychology just to be someone's friend."

He reluctantly agreed.

Deacon pulled Cody into his apartment without a word and closed the door softly. "Damn, I'm glad to see you," he said, taking her into his arms. He kissed her, then continued holding her for a moment. "I almost went crazy missing you today."

"Me too." She raised her eyes. "What's wrong? You look tense."

Deacon led her to the sofa, sat down, and pulled her onto his lap. "Oh, Alma Black gave me a new job today," he said, then went on to tell her about the men's shelter. "I'm going to have to start sleeping there tomorrow night."

She saw that he wasn't too pleased by the prospect. "When will I see you?"

"I don't have to work during the day," he said.

"We could be together then." He looked hopeful. "I go in at five in the afternoon to get things ready for the men. They have to be there before seven to claim a bed. I have to hang around till they leave the next morning." He sighed. "I guess we'll have to work out the party arrangements in my spare time."

"Katie and I will start addressing the envelopes when the invitations come in from the printer."

"What if nobody shows?" Deacon glanced away as he said it, not wanting her to see how worried he was over that possibility, even though he'd been so positive with Alma Black. "I mean, I've talked to a few of these people to make sure they can come, but how do we know the rest will make it?"

"We're asking them to RSVP as soon as possible, so we'll know pretty quick if they're coming."

He nodded. "I'm going to look like a fool if they don't show up."

Cody saw that he was genuinely concerned. "Let's just see what happens, Deacon," she said. "I'm sure it'll be okay."

He became thoughtful for a moment. "Do you know what it's like to be labeled a sex offender, Cody?" When she shook her head, he went on. "If somebody really wants to ruin you, that'll do it." He shook his head. "Sometimes I just don't think I can take any more. I can't help wondering what people are thinking. I constantly feel I need to prove myself, not only as a man but as a human being. I know Alma Black wants to humble me, but I'm too angry at the moment to be humbled. I feel somebody has really put the screws to me, and all I can think about is trying to get even."

"You're only human. I would be angry and hurt too."

He was glad she understood. "I don't know if I'm ever going to be able to bounce back from this, Cody," he confessed after a moment. "I mean, if I'd been busted for drugs or drunk driving, I would've been able to put my life back together one day, but this—" He paused. "This is a tough one. And I know I'll never be able to prove my innocence."

"The people who know you best will know you're innocent," she said softly. "I never doubted it for a moment."

He grinned suddenly. "That's 'cause you're crazy about me. Not everybody loves me as much as you do."

"Katie thinks you're innocent."

"Yes, but would she still feel that way if I didn't drive a Lotus?"

"You know she worships you."

"How about her mother?"

Cody looked into his eyes. Although he was smiling, she could sense that her answer meant a lot to him. "I told you once before: I've always loved you. It almost killed me when . . . when you left Calgary to make your fortune in Nashville."

"But not enough to make you come after me?"

"I figured I'd just be in the way."

He pushed her up from his lap and led her into the bedroom. He didn't want to rehash the past at the moment. He simply wanted to love her. "You could never be in my way."

They made love leisurely, taking time to reacquaint themselves with each other's body. Deacon kissed her eyelids, her ears, the delicate line of her jaw, then pressed his lips against the hollow of her throat, where her heart thumped out a soulful message. She returned his kisses eagerly, parting her lips wide to receive his greedy tongue. He entered her finally, and she rose up to meet him, and their sighs filled the room like a sweet song. Afterward, Deacon held her for a long time, until their breathing returned to normal.

"I love you, Cody," he said. "I didn't realize how empty I was inside until you came back into my life. Somehow we're going to have to make up for all those years we spent apart." He sounded sad.

Cody snuggled against him. "We will."

"We could have had babies by now. A ton of them. Remember how we both wanted a big family?"

"Yes, I remember. But I also remember how you wanted to be able to provide for them. You wanted our children to have more than you and your brothers had. You said you never wanted them to be ashamed of you or where they lived or how they dressed. Those are the things I remember most, Deacon."

He didn't seem to be listening. "It almost killed me when you dumped me," he said. "For three days I ranted and raved and told myself I was better off without you. Finally, I calmed down and decided we needed to talk. I went to your house, but your parents told me you had already left for Durham. They wouldn't give me your address or phone number. They said they'd call the sheriff if I didn't leave you alone."

"I never knew," she said softly. And she hadn't. Since Deacon had done nothing to contact her, she had just assumed he had been somewhat relieved that he could concentrate on his career and go to Nashville sooner.

"Your mother came out onto the porch as I was leaving and told me they were just acting on your wishes. That you didn't want to see me again." He sighed as if the memory were still painful. "Anyway, I left for Nashville a week later. I figured if I could prove myself to you, become a success, then you'd change your mind and come running to me. My mother said—" He paused. "Well, it's not important now."

"What did your mother say?" Cody asked, stiffening in his arms at the mere thought of Eileen Brody.

"She told me you were used to nice things, and that if I really wanted to win you back, I should try my best to succeed."

"That sounds like something your mother would say," Cody said dully.

He glanced down at her. "What do you mean?"

Cody realized she had spoken without thinking. "Nothing. I don't think our parents realized how much we loved each other at the time."

"My mother didn't want us to split up, Cody. In fact, she offered to go to your parents several times and try to make them see reason. We both know how overprotective your parents were."

It irked her that he could be so blind where his mother was concerned. "That's because they were older. They worried more than most parents. They didn't want me to rush into anything."

He pondered it. "Anyway, my mother kept tabs on you for me. I had just signed up with Mary-Lou Sly's band as a permanent member when I heard you'd married a guy from Durham. Frankly, I think my mother was as broken up over the news as I was."

It took all she had to keep from blurting the truth to Deacon. The fact that she herself had a child and only wanted the best for her made her more sympathetic to Eileen Brody.

"I have to go," Cody said after a moment. "I don't want Katie to find me gone."

He chuckled and pulled her close. "I think your daughter is a lot smarter than you think."

"What do you mean?"

"Don't you think she suspects something is going on between us?"

Cody looked surprised. "She hasn't said anything."

"That doesn't mean she doesn't know. Why are you keeping it a secret from her?"

"I don't want her involved until I know for sure what's going to happen between us. I don't want to rush into anything."

"We've known each other since we were fifteen. I'd hardly call that rushing."

"Yes, but we don't know what's going to happen with the future."

"I know that I want to be with you always," he said soberly. "As soon as I get this mess behind me, I want us to talk about our future. As I said before, I don't want to drag you and Katie down with me. I don't want people saying cruel things to the two of you."

"I believe you're innocent, Deacon. I don't care what other people think."

"But you still sound hesitant. Why?"

She sighed. "I'm just not sure there's a place in your life for Katie and me," she said honestly. "You're on the road three hundred days out of the year. What are Katie and I supposed to do in the meantime?"

"There's one helluva house waiting for you in Memphis, Cody. It has everything but a bowling alley to entertain the two of you."

"I don't want to be 'entertained.' I want to live like a normal family."

"Touring is part of my job," he said. "I'm not exactly crazy about it myself, but that's the way it is, so I accept it. Besides, it pays well. You and Katie will have everything."

"I don't want 'everything.'"

He chuckled. "First I was too poor for you. Now I'm too rich."

"You were never too poor." She reached for her clothes, deciding now was not the time to discuss it. She needed time to think. Deacon kissed Cody one last time before she stepped out into the dimly lighted hallway. He didn't even have a chance to close his door before a noise from Ms. Vickers's apartment startled them both. The elderly woman peered out at them through a slit in the door.

"Ms. Vickers, what are you doing up?"

The woman closed her door, slid her chain free, then opened her door wider. "I heard a noise," she said. "Is something wrong?"

Cody's face flamed as Ms. Vickers continued to look from her to Deacon. As if it weren't incriminating enough being caught sneaking from Deacon's apartment after midnight, Deacon himself was bare from the waist up, wearing only tight jeans and nothing else. She wanted to crawl into a hole and die.

"Oh, Cody, you don't want to forget this," Deacon said. He reached inside and pulled out a plunger and handed it to her. "Thanks for hanging around and mopping up all that water."

Suddenly, the old woman looked anxious. "Is there a problem with the plumbing?"

"Yes, ma'am," Deacon said. "Toilet overflowed and flooded the bathroom floor. Naturally, I didn't have a plunger, so I had to go down and wake Cody." He turned to Cody. "I sure am sorry I had to drag you out of bed like this."

Cody took the plunger, but she refused to meet the look in his eyes. "Oh, that's okay," she said, trying to sound casual. "You'll let me know if you have any more problems?" She smiled at Ms. Vickers. "Good night now. Sorry we woke you." She turned for the stairs, clutching the wooden handle of the plunger as she went.

Deacon arrived at the men's shelter shortly before five P.M. the next day. A lanky man with red hair and a red beard greeted him at the door.

"Call me P. W.," he said, pumping Deacon's hand. "I used to be a big fan of yours."

Deacon arched one brow. "Used to be?"

The man blushed, and the freckles on his nose became more noticeable. "Well, you haven't put out anything new lately."

"Yeah, you're right," Deacon said. "How 'bout showing me around?" The last thing he wanted to discuss with the stranger was the demise of his career.

P. W. nodded and motioned him into the kitchen, where a metal table sat in the center of the room, surrounded by eight mismatched chairs. "We're responsible for feeding 'em," he said. "I usually try to have a meal on the table by eight. They don't eat till they shower and clean up."

"What if I don't know how to cook?"

"Ain't nothin' to it. Just open a few cans of beans. Throw some wieners in water to heat so they can have a hot dog." He opened various cabinets so Deacon could glance inside. "Everybody has to be in by seven o'clock sharp. No leaving after that, or they can't come back in. We don't want nobody sneaking in drugs or booze. No women or loud music allowed either."

"Sounds like a fun time," Deacon said, his voice laced with sarcasm.

P. W. grinned. "Yeah, well, we don't want them to have no fun anyway. We're just giving 'em a place to sleep." He paused reflectively. "You know, I think they gave you a bum rap."

Deacon glanced at the man in surprise. He was referring to his yearlong court battle and his sentence, of course. Deacon offered him a brief nod. "Why don't you show me the rest of the place now?"

The sleeping quarters consisted of crudely built bunk beds. The sheets were dingy, but P. W. swore they were clean. Worn blankets had been folded at the foot of each bed, and a sagging sofa on a threadbare rug provided a sitting area. Deacon shook his head at the dismal sight. "Looks bad," he said.

P. W. shrugged. "It ain't the Hilton, but it keeps 'em outta the rain. Come on, I'll show you the showers."

By the time Deacon got a look at the mildewed shower stalls, he was depressed. Unfortunately, the private room he was to share with P. W. wasn't much better. "What do these guys do for entertainment?" he asked. "There's not a TV or radio in the place." He had already decided he would have preferred the rain on his head to spending a night inside these cold gray walls.

"It's all we can do to keep food in the place," P. W. told him. "We cain't afford much else." They were interrupted when somebody knocked on the front door. "That's somebody coming in now," he said. "We'd best get started."

The men arrived over the next hour, straggling in, hungry and dirty, some of them looking and smelling as though they hadn't bathed in weeks. While P. W. signed them in, Deacon led each man to a shower, handed him a bar of soap and a frayed towel. "You have to wash before you can eat," he told them. They nodded and did as they were instructed. Several large cardboard boxes held old clothes from which they could select something clean to wear. They rummaged through the boxes as eagerly as any child would on Christmas morning. Deacon thought of the two-hundred-dollar shirts hanging in his closet in Memphis that he had learned to take for granted.

"Well, what do you think?" P. W. asked Deacon once the men had fallen asleep for the night.

Deacon kicked off his boots and reclined fully clothed on the bed that was to be his. The mattress was lumpy, the sheets almost transparent from years of laundering, but they smelled clean. He wouldn't get any sleep tonight, he knew. "I think the whole thing is sad," he said after a moment. "This is one job I'll be glad to have behind me."

• • •

When Deacon knocked on Cody's front door shortly after ten the following morning, she ushered him into the kitchen for a cup of coffee. But when she handed it to him, he set the cup aside and took her in his arms instead.

"You look exhausted. Didn't you sleep last night?" she asked.

"Not much."

"Come lie down in my room."

He smiled tiredly. "Is that a proposition?"

She chuckled and led him through the hall to her bedroom at the back of the house. "No. I think you need sleep more than anything right now."

Deacon stepped through the doorway leading into her bedroom and gazed around. The oak furniture was old but well cared for. The vintage iron bed was covered with a powder-blue comforter that blended with the curtains and wallpaper and gave the room a cozy, welcoming look. "So this is where you sleep, huh?" He didn't have to ask. Her scent was everywhere. He walked to a small dressing table and gazed at the various bottles, opening each one and putting it to his nose.

Cody watched in amusement as Deacon opened her mascara and studied the wand. He checked out her lipstick and face powder as well. "Having fun?" she asked.

He grinned and nodded. "Remember when I used to sneak into your room, and we'd sit out on the roof and watch the stars?"

"My parents would have killed us if they had known."

He chuckled softly and moved toward her, taking in her appearance appreciatively. She was dressed in walking shorts and a knit shirt with a multicolor scarf tied carelessly around her neck. He reached for it and untied the knot slowly, and then, with the scarf still anchored at her neck, pulled, forcing her to step closer. He gazed into her eyes briefly before lowering his mouth to hers. The kiss was long and slow and very sensual.

"Remember the first night we were together?" he asked once he'd raised his face from hers.

Cody's heart caught in her throat. "Yes."

"I thought you'd been sent down from heaven. You were so beautiful. So delicate. I was afraid I'd hurt you."

"It felt too wonderful to hurt."

"I never forgot how you smelled or tasted. Never. I thought about it a lot when I first moved to Nashville. I used to lie awake at night and think about it. Sometimes—" He paused, wondering if maybe he was telling too much.

"Sometimes what?"

He met her gaze. "I used to pretend the person I was with was you. In the beginning, it didn't matter who I was making love to, because I kept my eyes closed and saw only you."

Cody glanced away. "Please don't tell me any more."

He pulled her close, knowing in his heart that he had wanted to hurt her with his confession. He'd obviously succeeded. Even though she had crushed all his hopes and dreams back then, he had still been able to function as a man. All those years he'd wanted to tell her as much, tell her how many women *hadn't* rejected him over the years. How many women would have *gladly* become his wife had he asked. Now he felt bad for having told her about those days. There was nothing sweet about revenge, not when it hurt the person dearest to him. Hurting her was like hurting a part of himself.

"I'm sorry," he whispered. He kissed her forehead, linked her hand in his, and led her to the bed, pulling her down with him. For a moment he simply gazed at her. "Anyway, I thought you were the most beautiful thing in the world the first time I made love to you. I knew then and there I wanted to spend the rest of my life with you. I even hoped you would become pregnant."

She was genuinely surprised. "You did? But what about your career and all your plans?"

"Those things were never as important to me as you were. Besides, if a man wants something bad enough, he's going to achieve it regardless."

"Sometimes a family can be more of a hindrance than a help, Deacon."

"Only if you let it." He paused. "It's like these guys who come into the shelter. They're full of hard-luck stories. They have an excuse for everything. They'd much rather sit around and tell you why they *can't* get a job than go out and try. Of course, not all of them are like that. A couple of them really want to succeed. They just don't believe in themselves enough."

"You could help them, Deacon."

Her statement baffled him. "What do you mean?"

"By telling them exactly what you just told me. Maybe if these men had someone who believed in them—"

"Forget it, Cody. I'm not good at that sort of thing."

"But who do they really have to help them?" she asked. "I mean, the shelter offers them a dry place to sleep and a plate of food, but what are you doing for their emotional and spiritual needs?"

"That's not my job. Besides, I don't have time to get involved in other people's troubles. I've enough of my own."

"I don't believe you can be that indifferent, Deacon," she said matter-of-factly. She struggled to sit up, but he chuckled and held her down. She squirmed. "You can put on this tough-as-nails act as long as you like, but I know you better than that. Inside, you really care."

He silenced her with a kiss. When he raised up he was grinning. "The only thing I care about right now is getting deep inside you, lady."

Cody almost shivered as his meaning sank in. She couldn't have resisted if she had wanted to, and she knew instinctively that Deacon wouldn't discuss his deep-down, personal feelings about his new job until he was darn good and ready. She would be there for him when he was.

Although Deacon was no longer holding her down, the stark, hungry look in his eyes prevented Cody from moving a muscle. Her belly warmed. His eyes never left her face as he undressed her, slowly and skillfully. Only when he had her completely naked did he look away. His own clothing joined hers on the floor, and Cody gazed appreciatively at the hard lines of his body. He was magnificent. She pressed her face against his wide chest, inhaled his scent, then licked the nubby brown nipples that peered out from the matted chest hair. Deacon closed his eyes and gave in to the sensations.

"Oh, Cody, you do the nicest things," he said.

They made love slowly; touching and tasting, whispering words of pleasure. Afterward Deacon held her for a long time. The house was quiet. "I've started writing again," he confessed after a moment.

Cody glanced up. "A new song?" When he nodded, she smiled. "Oh, Deacon, that's wonderful. What's it about?"

"I'm not sure yet. It started coming to me last night at the shelter. I couldn't find any paper so I slipped into the kitchen and wrote some of it out on a paper towel. I think it's going to be about feelings. Anger. Regret. I feel as if I have to do something with them. I can't keep holding them in, or I'll explode. I've got to tell my side of the story now, despite what my attorney thinks, and the only way I know how to do it is in a song." He chuckled. "'Course, it may not sell worth a cuss."

Cody raised up on one elbow and gazed down at his face, relaxed but tired. "It'll be a great song, Deacon. When you feel strongly about something, it shows in your music. This may very well be the best thing you've ever written."

He was genuinely touched. "It's nice having someone believe in you." He closed his eyes, but as he drifted off to sleep he thought of the wretched souls who came to the shelter who had no one.

Nine

The next few days found them all busy addressing invitations. Deacon arrived back from the
shelter each morning and spent time on the
telephone with agents and business managers,
and with the celebrities themselves who planned
to attend. Even with the short notice, most of
them were able to fit it into their schedules.
Those who knew Deacon best knew he'd been
treated unfairly by the Tennessee courts and
felt the event could get his career cranked up
again. So not only was it a way to build a cancer
research center for children, it was a way to
help a fellow entertainer and a friend.

"Country-music people are some of the most
kind-hearted people you ever met," he told
Cody, truly touched by the response. "Most of
them come from humble beginnings, and they've
never forgotten it."

Once the invitations had been mailed, Cody
began planning the event. She called a caterer
friend of hers and together they put together
an impressive menu of hors d'oeuvres. In the

meantime, Deacon, his manager, and his attorney discussed the upcoming press conference.

Although both men offered to fly in, Deacon refused. "I don't want it to look staged," he told them in a conference call. "My landlady said I could hold it in her living room, so we plan to keep it simple. I only want a few reporters." Before they hung up, Deacon's business manager insisted he attend to the ever-increasing stack of fan mail that he'd avoided over the months. Although he employed a staff to see to his mail and answer with a glossy, black-and-white postcard of himself, he had dismissed the crew when some of his fan mail had become nasty due to the case. One deranged soul had scared them all by sending a mock letter bomb. Although a group of security people examined all incoming mail now, Deacon continued to let it pile up unanswered in his agent's office.

"I think you should take a look at it," his manager said. "As a matter of fact. I was planning to send it to you by truck this week. You can't let a few bad letters keep you from your fans."

Deacon finally gave in. "You can go ahead and send it, but I don't know when I'll have a chance to look at it." He wasn't sure he was ready. He knew people thought he took his fans for granted, but nothing could have been farther from the truth. He and his band members may not have always given careful thought to what they said and did, especially in the early days, but he had taught his boys that their fans were their customers and the customer was always right.

Now he wondered how many of those customers he'd alienated. All he'd ever wanted to do was write music, put tunes to the lyrics crowding his head. In the beginning it had been fun touring all over the world singing his songs. Nobody had listened to him while he was growing up in Calgary as a mill worker's son. But they listened to Deacon Brody, the star—the man in tight pants and eel-skin boots. He only hoped people still wanted to hear his songs when his legal problems were over.

When the day of the news conference arrived the following week, Cody awoke to a yardful of television and news reporters. Vans and cars lined the normally quiet street, and her sidewalk was littered with equipment. Although the news conference was set for ten o'clock, Cody had to admit everyone much earlier so they could set up.

Deacon arrived for the press conference wearing skintight jeans, a flashy western-style shirt, and his famous eel-skin boots. A gold-nugget cross dangled from his left ear. Cody, standing away from the crowd, was as awed as the rest of them by his presence. This was Deacon Brody, the star. He was imposing and larger than life, and his cocky swagger suggested he thought rather highly of himself. There was little resemblance between this man and the one who'd held her naked body close to his the morning before and told her how much he needed her. This man was little more than a stranger. He glanced her way before he took a seat at the microphones, winked once, then gave his attention to the roomful of reporters.

Bulbs flashed in his face and microphones

were shoved under his chin as Deacon read the statement he and his attorney had prepared concerning the charity event he was planning. Once finished, he opened the floor for questions. One magazine editor asked if he would name some of the celebrities he'd invited to the upcoming benefit. He replied with an impressive list.

So far, so good, Cody thought.

Another reporter stepped forward. "Mr. Brody, can you tell us why you're suddenly so interested in doing something for this community, when you haven't lifted a finger in the past?"

"Mr. Brody, isn't it true you're only doing this because you want to try and restore your career?"

"Mr. Brody, have you begun your community service work yet?"

"Are you bitter about the sentence you were given, Mr. Brody?"

"Have you had any contact with the minor who was the subject of your yearlong court battle?" someone else asked.

Deacon visibly tensed, but he sat there and waited until the questions had died down, staring coldly at the crowd before him. "I did not call you here to discuss my court case," he said. "I think, in the past year, I've answered enough questions regarding that incident. I would like to get on with my life now, if it's at all possible. I don't want to be remembered as the man who got caught with a minor in his hotel room. There's more to me than that. If I can't prove my innocence, I would at least like to prove my worthiness. Now, since you obviously have no interest in the benefit I'm planning, I'm going to close this conference."

"Mr. Brody, wait!" Another reporter stepped forward and introduced himself. He was a small man with unusually dark features and eyes like a weasel's. "I'm Miles Fairchild," he began as Deacon was unhooking the microphone pinned to his shirt.

"I know who you are, Mr. Fairchild," Deacon told the man, trying to keep his anger in check. "If it hadn't been for that lousy tabloid you write for, the truth surrounding my conviction might have leaked out. Don't tell me you're here looking for facts. You certainly don't print them in your paper."

The man looked both surprised and embarrassed. "Mr. Brody, I assure you our paper is as concerned with the truth as the rest of these good people."

Cody stood frozen at the back of the room, listening to the heated exchange between the two men. She knew enough about the tabloid the reporter represented to know it wasn't always fair with the stories it printed. Its reporters had been dragged into court so many times, it wasn't funny. They'd been caught tampering with mail, bugging telephones, even going through people's trash if they had to in order to get a story. She was thankful she hadn't let Katie stay home from school after all.

"What is your question?" Deacon asked the man, his voice as cold as a winter wind.

"I'd simply like to know how the people of Calgary received you when you came back," he said, his eyes watching Deacon carefully. "I understand they wouldn't even rent to you. They were afraid to have you under the same roofs with their daughters. Isn't that true, Mr. Brody?"

Deacon's face turned beet red. He lunged for the man. "Why, you sorry sonofa—"

Cody pushed through the people separating her from Deacon. Reporters swung around in surprise, and the next thing she knew she was blinded by the flash of bulbs. Squinting, she groped her way through the crowd, toward Deacon. She grabbed him only a split second before he reached the man. "Don't," she said. "That's exactly what he's hoping you'll do." Deacon glanced at her in surprise while the bulbs continued to flash in their faces. Finally, he calmed down.

Cody glared at the reporter. "Your statement is untrue, Mr. Fairchild," she said, "just as everything else you print. I wasn't afraid to rent to Mr. Brody. I know he's completely innocent of the crime for which he was accused. He's incapable of committing such an act. If I didn't believe in him, I would never have let him under the same roof with my daughter."

"Who the hell are you?" the reporter asked.

"I'm his landlady, Cody Sherwood Cox. Mr. Brody and I are old friends, and I'll be more than happy to vouch for his good character." The man glanced at his notes, then fixed her with a knowing gaze.

"Aren't you the lady he dumped to run off and make a name for himself?" he asked.

This time it was Cody's turn to look surprised. The man had obviously done his research beforehand. She wondered if Maybelline Carter and some of her cronies had given him that information, and she couldn't help but wonder what else he knew.

"Mr. Brody never dumped me," she said

matter-of-factly. "I broke off the engagement because I knew how important his career was to him at the time."

"So you have a daughter, huh?" he asked. "Mind if I ask how old she is?"

She froze. "Yes, I do mind. I want my daughter kept out of this."

By the time the reporters had been ushered out, Cody was exhausted and more than a little shaken. She felt the tabloid reporter had sullied her living room. "How do you think it went?" she asked Deacon.

He looked tired as well. "It was as I expected it would be," he told her. "A few were interested in the benefit, but most of them were more interested in rehashing my trial. My lawyer tried to prepare me for the worst. I'm just glad Katie wasn't here to witness it."

"Me too. Although I'm sure she'll read about it."

He pulled her into his arms. "This is exactly what I didn't want to happen," he said. "I never wanted to involve you and your daughter. I never wanted to drag you down with me."

"We're stronger than you think, Deacon." She only hoped she sounded more confident than she felt.

Maybelline Carter's house was located in the heart of Calgary's historic district, only a few short blocks from Cody's place. Deacon decided to stop by one afternoon on his way to the shelter. The woman who answered the door, Maybelline's mother, had to be approaching ninety. The two had lived together in that house for as long as he could remember.

"Is Maybelline in?" Deacon asked the shrunken woman who peered back at him from over a pair of thick, wire-rimmed glasses.

"Who's callin'?" the woman asked.

"Tell her it's Deacon Brody."

"Have a seat." She motioned him into the room.

Deacon found himself in an airless living room with low ceilings, where the smell of something sickeningly sweet clung to the cushions and throw pillows. A massive library table near the window had been turned into a shrine of sorts, loaded down with Elvis Presley memorabilia. This "altar" was as dust-free as anything you might find in an operating room. He remembered it from her office.

"Well, *this* is a surprise," a voice said, bringing Deacon off the sofa with a start. "My mother's getting to where she'll let anyone in the house these days."

Deacon couldn't help but smile at her emotionless tone. Maybelline hadn't changed one iota, except that she'd gotten wider. Her girth spanned the doorway. "Hello, Miss Carter," he said. "Mind if I have a minute of your time?"

"Kinda late for you to be asking that question, since you're already making yourself at home in my living room. What do you want?"

"A favor."

"When Hades freezes over, Mr. Brody."

"I've nobody else to turn to, Miss Carter, and this is important." She looked unmoved. "If you won't do it for me, would you do it for the people of Calgary?"

She looked impatient. "Do *what*, boy?"

He briefly filled her in on his plans for raising funds for the children's cancer center. "Not only will this center give hope to sick children," he said, "but it will offer job opportunities to those who don't wish to spend their lives in a textile plant."

"There's nothing wrong with working in the textile plant," she said. "My parents worked there till they were old enough to retire."

"Then you obviously forgot the speech you gave us in high school when you told the senior class we should strive to do better than those who came before us."

Maybelline looked surprised. "Yes, well, I was always making speeches back then. Folks accused me of being long-winded." She gave a snort. "Brody, I know why you're doing this. You're just trying to pull that career of yours out of the mud."

"Yes, ma'am," he said, and was awarded with another look of surprise, this one for his honesty. "But if I can help someone else in the process, then at least I haven't harmed anyone."

"So what's that got to do with me?"

"Well, since there isn't a nice hotel in town, I was hoping you'd put up a friend of mine for a couple of nights."

"I won't have any drug addicts under my roof, and I don't approve of folks using alcohol either."

"That's why I chose you, Miss Carter. This man is a good Christian fellow and—"

"Well, that's all fine and dandy, but I ain't got no time to be playing hostess to some hotshot celebrity friend of yours. You'll have to find someone else." She went for the door. "Now, if you don't mind, I've got things to do."

"Yes, ma'am." He crossed the room and made

his way through the open door, pausing once to thank her. "I appreciate your time anyway, Miss Carter. I'm sure I can find suitable lodgings for my friend." When he mentioned the man's name, Maybelline almost fainted. He was her favorite singer.

"Maybe you've heard of him."

Maybelline's mouth dropped to her chest. "*He's* coming to Calgary?"

"Yes, ma'am. Just talked with him this morning, as a matter of fact."

Maybelline took a moment to compose herself. "Oh my, where are my manners?" she said all of a sudden. "I didn't even offer you something cool to drink. Would you like a glass of lemonade before you go?"

Three days later, Cody answered the bell and found Miles Fairchild on her doorstep. "What do you want?" she asked tersely.

"Aren't you going to invite me in?"

Cody glared back at him. "Give me one good reason," she said, resisting the urge to slap the smug look off his face as she remembered all he'd said to Deacon at the press conference, all he'd done to destroy Deacon's career during his trial.

"One good reason?" he asked. "Is the name Hank Cox good enough?"

Cody knew a moment of sheer horror. Her legs suddenly felt weak, as though they might collapse any moment. She noticed it was after five. Deacon would have already left for the shelter. Katie had gone to an early movie with a girlfriend. "Yes, come in," she said, standing back so he could pass through the open door.

• • •

Deacon pulled into the parking lot of the shelter, put his car in gear, and was about to turn off the ignition when P. W. hurried out, waving a piece of paper. Deacon put his window down. "What is it?"

"You just had a phone call," P. W. told him. "The guy says it's urgent. He wants you to meet him at the Country Squire Restaurant right away."

Deacon frowned, wondering what it could possibly be about. "Who, P. W.?" he said. "What man?"

P. W. glanced at the piece of paper. "His name's Cox. Henry Cox."

The Country Squire Restaurant was almost empty when Deacon walked through the front door twenty minutes later. With the exception of a redheaded waitress and a well-dressed man in a wheelchair, Deacon was the only one there. He slid onto a stool at the counter, ordered a cup of coffee, and fixed his gaze on the door, hoping that Henry Cox would not make him wait long. The waitress handed Deacon his coffee, almost spilling it as she did so. She knew who he was, despite the fact that he still wore his sunglasses. He appreciated it, though, when she walked away instead of asking for an autograph as folks usually did. He wasn't in the mood for conversation at the moment. He merely wanted to know what Henry Cox wanted with him, of all people.

"Mr. Brody?"

Deacon jumped at the sound of his name and swung his head around. Nobody had come through the door. He glanced at the man in the wheelchair, and the man nodded and motioned him over. So he wasn't going to get out of signing autographs after all, he thought. "Yeah?" His voice sounded cold in his own ears.

"Won't you join me?" the man said politely.

"Thanks, but I'm expecting someone."

The man smiled. "You've found him, Mr. Brody. I'm Henry Cox."

Deacon sank into the chair, but his gaze remained fixed on the man and his wheelchair. "*You're* Henry Cox?" he said, wanting to make sure he'd understood correctly. "You used to be married to Cody Sherwood? You're Katie's father?"

The smile faded from the other man's face. "Yes, I was married to Cody for a while," he said. He paused and indicated the wheelchair. "You're probably wondering about my injury," he said, as though to change the subject. "Most people are curious, although they try not to show it. I am completely paralyzed from the waist down."

"Cody didn't tell me."

The man chuckled. "That doesn't surprise me. She never thought of me as being handicapped, no matter how many times I felt sorry for myself. I would never have become the successful architect I am today without her. She refused to let me give up." He sighed. "Actually, it's not as bad as it sounds. My house is perfectly equipped to handle my disability, and I make good money designing houses for other disabled people. My van enables me to get to and from my office every day, so I am able to support myself very well." He chuckled. "Of course, that's about *all* I can do, if you know what I mean." He glanced at the young waitress as though to drive the statement home. "Except for listening to music and reading books. I'm a devoted fan of mysteries and horror novels. And, Cody, bless her heart, always sends me books at Christmas and birthdays."

Deacon wondered why the man was telling him so much, but he didn't wish to appear rude. Henry Cox had a reason for wanting to see him, and he was curious to know why. "So how long ago did you hurt yourself?" he asked.

"Oh, it was a childhood accident, Mr. Brody. One I received from diving into shallow water from a fishing pier. Crazy what a ten-year-old boy will do to impress his friends, isn't it?"

Cody debated whether to answer the door when she heard the bell peal out. She didn't want to see or talk to anyone. Her eyes were still red from crying, and she was trembling from head to toe. Of course, she had waited until she'd thrown that sorry reporter out before she'd broken down, before she'd hurled herself onto her bed and sobbed into her pillow for an hour. Her day of reckoning had come, and she was going to have to pay the consequences. Still, the shame and regret of it all was a terrible thing to have to live with for the rest of her life.

The bell sounded again. Surely it wasn't Katie back already, she thought. Katie, who was always late and who usually called to see if she could stay out just a bit longer. She paused at the door. "Who is it?" she asked, trying to make her voice sound light despite the heaviness inside.

"It's me, Cody," Deacon said from the other side. "Open the door."

"Deacon?" Cody felt her heart slam to her throat. She sniffed and wished she had a tissue. "But why aren't you at the shelter?" she called back, knowing she was stalling. Trying to buy time. What was *he* doing there?

"Open the damn door, Cody, or I'll kick it in."

Cody reached for the dead bolt with trembling fingers. His voice was deadly. He knew. He knew! Worse, he hadn't learned it from her. She should have been the one to tell him. She had *planned* to be the one to tell him all along, from the beginning actually, but the time had never seemed right. He'd had so much on his mind. So many problems. She took a deep breath and cracked open the door, but nothing could have prepared her for the look on his face.

Deacon shoved the door the rest of the way open, then kicked it shut behind him. It slammed loud enough to shake the house. Cody took a step back, startled by the murderous look in his eyes. He closed the distance between them, looking as though he might very well strike her.

"Just who the hell do you think you are?" he demanded between gritted teeth. He balled his fists at his sides.

She almost flinched at the sound of his voice. Never in her life had she seen him so angry, not even that night thirteen years ago when she'd told him she never wanted to see him again. "Deacon, wait. I can explain. I had planned to tell you." The fear in her heart was evident in her voice.

He grabbed her by the wrist and jerked her closer, so close, she could see herself in his eyes. "When, Cody? When were you going to tell me I am Katie's real father?"

Ten

The room seemed to spin around her once he'd said the words, once he'd tossed the accusation in her face. For years she had imagined this scene, wondered what he would do if he ever found out. Even when she and Henry had planned the whole thing, and Henry had warned her the day might indeed come, despite her assurances to the contrary. She had never expected to see Deacon Brody again.

Cody licked her lips now, wondering when her mouth had gone dry. "How did you find out?" she asked. "Did Mr. Fairchild visit you?"

"I just had a nice long conversation with Henry Cox. Your *ex-husband*. The man you led me to believe was Katie's father. The man who is *incapable* of being anybody's father."

Cody tried to still her trembling hands by clasping them together in front of her. "Deacon, I know you're not going to believe me, but I wanted to tell you so many times. I still have the letters I wrote you back then. It's really a relief that you know because—"

"Cut the small talk, Cody. Just give me the truth."

"It's a long story."

"You and I aren't leaving this room until you tell me."

"May I sit down?" Her legs were trembling so badly, she knew she had to either sit or fall.

"Go ahead." He indicated the sofa with a nod, then released her abruptly.

Cody walked to the couch and sat on the edge stiffly. She massaged her wrist where the imprint of his fingers still showed. "I don't know where to begin."

"Why don't you begin where we left off?" he suggested, crossing his arms over his wide chest. "Begin the night you dumped me."

"I never wanted to break up with you. I only did it because I loved you. I loved you more than I loved life itself, Deacon. You have to believe that."

"I'm not sure what to believe right now. But go on."

His words hurt, but it was no less than she deserved, she supposed. "Deacon, I wanted to marry you from the time I was fifteen years old," she said. "It's all I thought about in high school. But we were so young, for heaven's sake, barely graduated. We didn't even have good jobs." The look on his face told her she was getting nowhere with him.

"The simple truth is, I didn't want you to be like your father. I didn't want you to grow old before your time doing mill work, and I knew if you stayed in Calgary, that's where you'd end up. I didn't want to have to rake and scrape to feed our children like your poor parents had to do with you and your brothers. And I knew you'd be miserable living like that." Her eyes shimmered with tears. "I was afraid you'd end up hating me." She glanced away. "Of course, I had no way of knowing I was pregnant the night I broke off with you. When I found out, I wrote you this long letter, then called your mother for your address, but—"

"But what?"

"Well, she told me how you were practicing day and night to audition with Mary-Lou Sly's band and that you were very nervous—" She paused. "I didn't want to do anything to jeopardize that."

"So why didn't you do something once I was hired on?"

"I did, Deacon. I mailed the letter to you as soon as I'd heard you got the job. I didn't hear anything for weeks. Then one day the letter came back marked 'address unknown.' The next thing I know, you're touring with Mary-Lou's band and the tabloids are filled with pictures of her new love.

"It was all hype and nothing more," he told her. "I never laid a hand on her till after I found out about you and Henry Cox. Which leads me to the next question: How does *he* fit into all this?"

"I was staying with Henry's family at the time. Waiting for classes to begin. My parents thought it would be a good idea for me to go early and have them show me around. The Coxes were old friends of my parents." She paused. "Henry and I became good friends. He showed me around, and I think I helped him in return. He was pretty depressed because, well, he couldn't do all the things other kids could do." She sighed, and she could feel the tears sliding down her cheeks. "At the time it seemed the logical thing to do—for Henry and me to get married, that is. I told him everything, and even though he encouraged me to go to you with the truth, I couldn't."

"Do you have any idea how that made me feel, Cody? To learn you were married, with a baby on the way? I felt like the world's greatest fool. I couldn't imagine how you could have met some guy and gotten pregnant that fast, unless you'd been seeing him all along."

"I know how it must've looked, Deacon, and I'm sorry, but I didn't think I had any other choice at the time."

He was unmoved by her apology. "What did Henry's parents think of the whole thing?"

"His parents treated me like a daughter. When Henry and I told them my situation and the solution we'd come up with, they accepted it fully. They knew I wasn't trying to saddle their son with the responsibility. I was simply looking to give my baby a name." The tears fell freely now. "And like Henry himself said, it wasn't likely he'd marry or have children. Mr. and Mrs. Cox have always treated Katie like a grand-daughter, and they were all very good to me when I lost my parents so close together."

"So then what?" Deacon asked. "Did you just dump poor ol' Henry too, after you got what you needed from him?"

It hurt her to know he thought so little of her. "Actually, he dumped me." When Deacon looked surprised, she went on. "We stayed to-gether until I graduated college. Katie was four by then, and we figured nobody would ask questions when I moved back to Calgary. Which they didn't, because I told them Katie was born prematurely. And since nobody had ever seen Henry in person, they had no idea he couldn't—" She blushed. "You know."

"Make love to you?" he ground out. She nodded. "So if it was all so wonderful, why'd he dump you?"

Her eyes flooded with fresh tears. "He didn't want to be a burden to me." She laughed and wiped the tears away. "He said I'd done such a good job of making him believe in himself that he no longer needed anyone around to see after him. He wanted me to find a man and lead a normal life. I wanted to stay, but I was afraid he would think I did it out of pity. So I moved back in with my parents and filed for a divorce."

Deacon sighed heavily and raked his hands through his hair. "So what about Katie? She thinks Henry is her father?"

Cody's voice was barely audible when she spoke. "Yes."

He felt as though she'd struck him. "How *could* you, Cody? How could you bear my child and never tell me? How could you lie to your own daughter about something that important?"

She choked on a sob. "I only did what I thought was best. I was nineteen years old at the time, Deacon. Maybe it wasn't the *perfect* decision. But it was the only logical one at the time. Since then, I suppose I've felt compelled to live with it. Besides, Henry has always treated Katie well."

"Maybe so, Cody, but he hasn't played an active part in her life, has he?"

"It's not easy for him to make the trip from Durham alone. He comes Thanksgiving and Christmas, and he has never missed Katie's birthday. He calls her often." She sniffed. "And Katie loves him."

"So you're going to spend the rest of your life lying to the girl?" he said.

"No. I planned to tell her several years back, but then my father got sick and died. We hadn't really had time to recover from that, when my mother died. Then I was concerned with renovating this house so I could make a living and—"

"You've got an excuse for everything, don't you?"

"I'm not trying to make excuses. I'm trying to make you understand, Deacon."

"Well, I don't. I don't understand how you could just toss me aside all those years ago, and I will never understand how you could keep my daughter a secret from me. I had a right to know, Cody. A legal and a moral right to know about my own child." He made his way to the door.

"Where are you going?"

He turned and glared at her. "I'm going to work. The shelter. I'll come back for my clothes in a couple of days."

"You're moving out?"

"Yeah. I can live at the shelter. I just want to put in my hours and get out of this town once and for all."

She stood and hurried toward him. "But what about the benefit? And all the people we've invited?"

"I'll be here for that." He opened the door. "In the meantime, send the bills to me at the shelter." He stepped out into the hall and closed the door behind him.

• • •

When Katie walked through the front door at three-thirty, she found her mother sitting at the kitchen table, staring into a cold cup of coffee. She didn't even look up when the girl came into the room.

"Mom?"

Cody jumped at the sound of her daughter's voice. "Oh, I'm sorry, honey, I didn't hear you come in. How was school?"

Katie took a seat at the table and studied her mother's face. "What's wrong, Mom? You've been crying. Did something happen?"

Cody reached across the table and took her daughter's hand. Lord, she loved the girl. She had never wanted to do anything to hurt her. But she knew she had to prepare the child for the story Miles Fairchild would write. "Katie, we have to talk," she said.

The day of the benefit dawned bright. Cody barely had time to shower and change before the doorbell began to ring. The first group arrived in a large van containing folding tables. Cody showed them a diagram of where the tables and chairs were to be placed on the back lawn. Tiny white lights were strung through the trees and torches were placed sporadically around the yard, both to add a festive look and to keep the mosquitoes away.

The day was taxing to Cody, who asked Katie to answer the door and direct traffic while she saw to food preparations. Although a caterer was handling the hot food, Cody was providing cheese, vegetable, and fruit trays. She and Katie had been cleaning vegetables for three days. A group of security men arrived, combed the area, attached extra padlocks to the tall wrought-iron gates, and promised to be back shortly in uniform. Although a handful of celebrities were planning to spend the night in Calgary at various private homes, most of them were flying out after the benefit. Extra personnel had been added at the small airport in town to accommodate those with private planes; the rest of them would be shuttled from the Winston-Salem airport in a limo. Deacon himself had seen to the travel and housing arrangements.

True to his word, he had moved out of the apartment and into the shelter. Although he'd called Cody a couple of times to discuss the benefit and dropped by once to pick up several bags of fan mail his manager had sent, his tone had been abrupt and had not invited a personal discussion.

Katie's mouth had dropped almost to the floor when Cody had told her the truth about her birth.

"I had planned to tell you a long time ago," she told the girl, "but the time was never right. I'm sorry, Katie, truly sorry for deceiving you."

Katie had forgiven her, although Cody saw that the news had hit her rather hard. Even though she was excited at the thought of being the daughter of a big celebrity, she still felt an allegiance to Henry Cox. Henry himself had called, explaining to Cody he'd told Deacon the truth because Miles Fairchild from the tabloid had come around asking questions. He'd felt it was time Katie's biological father knew the truth.

"I don't like all this subterfuge, Cody," he'd

said. "You knew from the beginning how I felt about keeping Katie's parentage a secret. Her father deserved to know the truth. Besides, Mr. Fairchild isn't going to waste any time printing the story, now that he knows."

Henry was right, she knew.

Her guilt was enormous. She'd used Henry, lied to her daughter, and hurt Deacon considerably with her secrets, and now everything was out in the open. She only hoped Katie would not suffer too much over the deception and that one day Deacon could forgive her just a little bit. But that wasn't likely to happen right away. Deacon had been anything but forgiving on the phone. He felt she had deceived him not once but twice. And she wasn't sure she could ever forgive herself.

Reporters and newsmen were swarming the grounds by noon. The roads were blocked off, and the sheriff had sworn in two dozen deputies to keep order. Still, it looked as though every citizen in Calgary had found a spot along the road, where the sheriff had blocked off the area with yellow police tape. Inside the pink Victorian structure, it was no better. Cody could barely get from one room to the next without bumping into a dozen people. She was beginning to wonder if life would ever be quiet and normal again.

Bulbs flashed and a roar went up from the crowd as the celebrities begin to arrive shortly after seven, the women dressed in flowing gowns, the men in tuxedos. Cody wore a simple peach cocktail dress that fell several inches above her ankles. Although Deacon had sent her money for a gown, she'd returned it and made something suitable for Katie and herself on her antique sewing machine in what spare time she'd been able to find. She thought her daughter looked absolutely adorable in a long dress of eyelet cotton.

Deacon arrived at eight wearing a black tux, flanked by band members dressed much the same. Although his group had set up their equipment earlier, Cody had had very little chance to talk to the men. Now it was hard to think of anything to say with Deacon standing there looking so wonderful. Katie hurried up to him and they exchanged a warm hug, while Cody stood off to the side feeling completely left out. Deacon wouldn't even look at her, she noticed, and when Miles Fairchild stepped up to take a picture, his eyes turned menacing.

"How would you like to eat that thing?" Deacon asked. The man scrambled away before Deacon could get the chance to feed it to him.

By nine o'clock the party was in full swing. A long buffet table beneath a green and white canopy provided the fare: prime rib, veal, seafood dishes. The tables were draped in white. Candles flickered among vases of fresh flowers, while a small orchestra played beneath another canopy that had been set up for entertainment. The tiny white lights made the whole thing look like something out of a fairy tale, and it was all Katie could do to contain her excitement. When Deacon invited the girl to dance, Cody thought her daughter would drop into a dead faint on the spot. They danced to several tunes, chatting with each other as they did so, and Cody couldn't help but wonder what they were discussing.

She was vaguely aware that Maybelline had come up and was saying something to her.

Cody blinked at the large woman, who was draped in a black gown that was obviously meant to hide her extra weight.

"Cody, how nice you look this evening," the woman said, her chubby cheeks flushed with excitement.

Cody's voice was cool when she answered. "Thank you, Maybelline. I hope you're having a nice time."

"Wonderful. You can imagine how surprised I was when Mr. Brody asked me to let my favorite singer stay at my place. Well"—she paused and sucked in her breath—"the first thing I did was hire a painting crew. I can't afford it, of course, but there was no way he could have come when my walls needed painting so badly." She leaned closer. "I was sort of hoping Mr. Brody would reimburse me for the expense, if you know what I mean. He can certainly afford it."

"You'll have to discuss that with him," Cody said. "Now, if you'll excuse me, I have to see to our guests."

Dessert consisted of cherries jubilee and various fruits and cheeses. Coffee was set out in tall silver urns and waiters took orders for after-dinner cocktails. Cody tried in vain to catch Deacon alone. Finally, at eleven, he and his band took the stage.

"Good evening, ladies and gentlemen," Deacon said into the microphone. "I hope you are all having a good time." There was a murmur in the crowd and finally a brief applause. "You all know the reason you're here tonight, so I'll be brief. We've asked the administrator of Calgary General Hospital to attend—" Deacon paused and glanced toward an elderly man standing offstage. "Mr. Barnett, would you please come up to the microphone?"

Deacon waited until the man was beside him before he turned his attention back to the crowd. "When I was ten years old, my little sister contracted leukemia," Deacon said after a moment. "Back then, there wasn't a whole lot of hope to offer patients, especially in a place the size of Calgary, North Carolina. My sister died." He paused again. "I think part of me died at the same time. I grew hard and bitter. Since then, a lot of good things have happened to me. Of course, last year my life took a turn for the worse, and, once again, I became bitter. But I believe good things come to those who suffer hardship. Even though I have maintained my innocence for the crime for which I was accused last year, I was guilty of a lot of other things. Anybody who reads the tabloids is aware of them." There was laughter in the crowd. "But mostly, I was guilty of looking the other way when I saw people suffering. I didn't want to have to look at it anymore 'cause I figured I'd paid my dues by watching my sister die. I thought as long as I had enough money I would be protected against bad things. I just assumed it was somebody else's turn. But I was wrong. I can't keep my eyes closed anymore. And neither can you."

Deacon reached into his pocket for an envelope. "Your generosity tonight will make it possible for Calgary General to begin the cancer research center that was not available to my sister, Kimberly Brody." He swallowed and for a moment it looked as if he might get emotional. "Her life could not be saved, but I am hoping we can save other children." He cleared his throat and faced the man. "Mr. Barnett, I promised to match the funds raised tonight, and I've decided to do a little bit better than that. I would now like to present you with a check for five hundred thousand dollars. It isn't enough to build the center, but I promise to rally for the remaining funds."

There was a loud applause this time as the hospital administrator stood before the microphone and made a brief speech, thanking Deacon and his friends for their help, for opening their hearts and their pocketbooks to help children with cancer. He, too, looked near tears. Once the man stepped off the stage, Deacon resumed his place at the mike.

"A lot of you have asked me what I've been doing the last year," he said once the clapping had died down. "I guess the only thing I can say is that I've been learning lessons. I learned a helluva lot during my trial. I learned that your real friends will stick with you no matter what, that they'll continue to believe in you no matter how incriminating the evidence. I am lucky to have a number of . . . good friends and devoted fans," he added, thinking of the fan mail sitting back in his room at the shelter, of the supportive letters he read at night after everyone fell asleep. He chuckled. "I am also unfortunate enough to have a few enemies in this business who don't believe in me. I will never be able to convince these people of my innocence. So I've decided if I can't prove my innocence, I can at least . . . prove my worthiness." It was a very personal speech for Deacon, as evidenced by the numerous pauses. Cody blinked back tears as she listened.

"Some of you know I've spent the past weeks working in a shelter for homeless men. I remember hearing a saying once about a man who felt bad for having no shoes until he saw a man with no feet. I thought I was bad off till I saw these men who had no homes." He cleared his throat, and it was obvious he was, once again, trying to get his emotions under control. "Anyway, working at the shelter has forced me to take a close look at my own life. I'd like to sing a song I wrote one night while I was there and couldn't sleep. I titled the song 'I Got Lost Along the Way.'"

The crowd went quiet as Deacon's band started the tune, a slow number about a man who'd started out poor in life and made his riches, then forgot who he was and where he'd come from. It was a song about the man's day of reckoning and the hard lessons he'd learned along the way. It was about a man who had found success but lost his soul. It was about a man who was desperately trying to find something good left within himself. It was a painful song, but beautifully poignant at times. Standing in the shadows, Cody felt her heart break into a million pieces, and she knew by the silence in the room that Deacon's audience had been moved as well. Even Maybelline Carter seemed touched by the words. When the song came to an end, there was an explosion of applause, and the audience gave Deacon a standing ovation.

Cody hurried inside the house and into her bedroom, where she cried in private before coming back out. And then the beautiful people began leaving, and all that was left behind was the smell of flowers and perfume. The dishes were cleared and packed into a box, the tables stripped of their cloths and folded, ready to be packed into the van the next day. It was after two o'clock in the morning before the caterer and her staff left. Cody sent Katie to bed, turned off the lights, and walked out onto the front porch for a breath of fresh air. She had barely closed the door behind her before she realized she was not alone. She sought and found Deacon's profile in the dark. "I thought you'd already left."

"I came back to say good-bye."

She swallowed. "Good-bye?"

He stood and closed the distance between them. "I'm leaving for Memphis tonight. My band is waiting back at the motel."

"I see."

"I wanted to talk to you about Katie before I left."

"Katie?" She knew a moment of intense disappointment. What had made her think he could possibly be interested in a reconciliation with her? "What do you want to discuss about her?"

"I want her to come to Memphis when school's out. For the summer."

Cody tensed. "She's never been away for that length of time, Deacon. I'm not sure—"

"You can fight me on this, of course," he said, "but I'll drag you into court if I have to. She's my daughter too. You've kept her from me for twelve years. I don't think one summer is asking too much."

"I'm not trying to fight you, Deacon, I'm only trying to decide what's best for Katie."

"If that were true, you would have told her about me a long time ago."

Anger flared inside her. Wasn't it bad enough she had to face her own guilt every time she looked into her daughter's face? How long did she have to suffer? Did Deacon mean to rub her nose in it for the rest of her life? "When should I have told her, Deacon?" she asked abruptly. "When you and your band were dragged into court all those times for destroying hotels? When the paper mentioned your all-night parties that were little more than orgies? Perhaps I should have sat her down when the police confiscated drugs on one of your band members. Is that when I should have told Katie who you were?"

"I've never taken drugs in my life, and you know it. And most of the other stuff was rumors written by jerks like Miles Fairchild."

"I had no way of knowing that, and neither did Katie. Frankly, I was embarrassed to tell her." She paused and sighed wearily. "But now that she knows who you are, she will naturally want to spend time with you. Once you can convince me she will be properly cared for, maybe we can work something out."

"I'll care for her personally," he said. "I won't be touring until next fall, so I plan to be home all summer." When Cody didn't answer right away, he went on. "I don't expect you to make a decision tonight," he said. "But I do expect one. You are *not* going to keep her from me anymore."

Cody didn't miss the anger in his voice. He could make life hard on her if he wanted. "I'll talk to Katie," she said after a moment, "but you're going to have to try and act civil if you expect me to send my daughter to you for any length of time."

He stepped closer. "*Our* daughter."

"*I* carried her for nine months. *I* raised her."

"And *I* planted her in your belly," he shot back. "Don't ever forget that, Cody. It may not mean anything to you, but it means a helluva lot to me." He started to walk away, then paused, raking his eyes over her once more. "Katie has my telephone number. She can call me collect anytime. In the meantime, you'll be hearing from me."

Cody watched him cross the yard and climb into his car. Her heart was still pounding loudly in her chest as he started the engine and drove away. "You'll be hearing from me," he'd said. Cody knew what that meant. Deacon Brody was going to make her pay dearly for her deception.

Eleven

If Cody had thought Deacon planned to contact her personally about seeing Katie, she was sorely mistaken. Two weeks after his departure, she received a letter from his attorney outlining future visitations with Katie, which included three months that summer. They had also worked out child-support payments and a trust fund for Katie's education, both of which were extremely generous. Yet, Cody was nervous about the whole thing. If Deacon chose to get nasty, she did not have the financial means to fight him. She responded to the attorney's letter right away, telling him that she would agree to two weeks' visitation as soon as school let out for the year, but that she felt her daughter needed time to adjust to everything before she spent an entire summer with her father.

Katie spoke to Deacon on the telephone several times a week, and the calls sometimes lasted a couple of hours. Cody had no idea what they could possibly be discussing at such length, but she didn't dare interfere. Guilt told her

Deacon had every right to get to know his daughter now.

"Deacon is going to start recording his new song this week," Katie told Cody one morning. "His manager says it's going to be the best thing he's ever done."

Cody took in the information in silence. The newspapers were full of talk these days about the new and improved Deacon Brody. The talk-show hosts were begging him to appear on their programs, and he did agree to interviews with a couple of them, explaining how he'd been forced to come to terms with himself over the past year.

Cody was watching one of the shows with Katie one night when the host asked Deacon about rumors that he had a daughter in Calgary, North Carolina, and he acknowledged the fact.

"But why have you kept it so secret?" the woman asked. "You're not ashamed of her, are you?"

Cody held her breath for his answer.

"Of course I'm not ashamed," Deacon said abruptly. "Her mother and I kept it quiet because we wanted the girl to have a normal life."

"And do you have a relationship with your daughter's mother?" the interviewer asked.

"We both want the best for our daughter," he said without elaborating.

Cody left Katie to watch the show alone, deciding it was just too painful.

The last few days of school passed much too quickly for Cody as she tried to prepare Katie for her visit with Deacon. Cody purchased a couple of outfits for Katie, using her own money to buy them, simply because she refused to cash the checks Deacon had sent. Instead, she put them into an account for her daughter to use at a later date. Besides, she'd provided well enough for Katie all her life, and she would continue to do so.

Deacon arrived on the first day of summer vacation, and the sight of his red Lotus sent Katie flying from her chair and out into the front yard, where she threw herself into her father's arms. Wearing a brave smile, Cody watched the scene from the doorway. Inside, her heart was breaking. For twelve years she'd had Katie all to herself. Now she was going to have to share her. That meant holidays as well, she reminded herself. Deacon would naturally want to spend some of them with his only child. Her insides ached at the thought. She could not imagine spending a single Thanksgiving or Christmas without her daughter. But none of these thoughts showed on her face as she kissed Katie good-bye and watched the Lotus disappear down the street.

The following two weeks crept by slowly for Cody. The only good thing was the fact that she had a lot of bookings for the month of June. Much to her relief, there had been no more cancellations, and when Maybelline Carter called to arrange a graduation party for her niece, Cody went all out for the event. She had several bridal showers, two wedding receptions, a surprise birthday party, and a fiftieth anniversary party for an elderly couple—along with the regular monthly garden club meetings and those of various other civic groups. Business was definitely picking up, and she wasn't so strapped for money. Which was why, she convinced herself, she wasn't in a hurry to rent out Deacon's old apartment. In fact, she couldn't even bring herself to go inside.

She was a wreck, and she knew it. She couldn't sleep, and she couldn't eat. During the night she was wound up tighter than a rubber band; by day she was so tired she couldn't concentrate. She missed her daughter, she missed Deacon. Her heart was broken.

The day Katie was to arrive back, Cody cleaned the house, prepared her daughter's favorite meal, and took a lot of time fixing herself up. She had lost weight, and there were dark circles beneath her eyes that makeup couldn't quite hide. Sitting on the sofa in the front parlor, she felt her heart leap to the back of her throat when Deacon's red car pulled into the driveway. She jumped up and raced out the door to meet her daughter.

Katie looked fit and tan and happy as her mother enfolded her in her arms. Cody was vaguely aware of Deacon pulling luggage from the trunk of his car. "I'm so glad you're home," she whispered into her daughter's ear. Already her eyes were filling with tears.

"Jeeze, Mom," Katie said. "I only went away for two weeks. You act as if I just spent five years in Angola with the Peace Corps."

Cody laughed at her emotional display, stepped back, and took a closer look at the girl. "You look wonderful. Is that a new outfit?"

Katie nodded and shot an adoring look at Deacon. "Dad bought it for me."

'Dad'? Cody glanced at Deacon, and saw him

smiling proudly at the girl. He met Cody's gaze, and although his smile faded slightly, his look didn't turn contemptuous, as it had the past couple of times. "Would you like to come inside for a moment?" she asked. "For something cold to drink?"

He nodded. "Yeah, sure." Then, to his daughter, "We'll need a crane to carry all these bags." He winked and carried the oversize suitcases up the steps.

"You bought new luggage?" Cody asked her daughter.

Katie giggled. "We had to. For all the clothes Dad bought me."

Cody's smile was forced. "I see."

"Did anybody call?" Katie asked the minute they walked through the front door.

"The phone hasn't stopped ringing all day. I put your messages on your bed."

"Excuse me," Katie said to Deacon. "I'd better check in case something important happened while I was gone." She hurried from the room.

Deacon set the luggage down and followed Cody into the kitchen, where she poured him a tall glass of iced tea. She handed it to him, careful to avoid touching him in any way. "Sounds like Katie had fun," she said.

He drank the tea. "Does that bother you?"

His question surprised her. "Why should it?"

"You don't sound happy. It's the clothes, isn't it?"

"I can't afford to buy all those things for her, Deacon. Until now, her tastes have been rather modest. I saw the new sneakers on her feet, and I know they cost over a hundred dollars. What am I supposed to do when she grows out of them, and all I can afford are dime-store specials?"

"I sent you a hefty check that would have more than covered a new pair of shoes, Cody. What did you do with the money?"

She felt her temper flare. "Oh, the usual," she said, her voice tinged with sarcasm. "I bought designer lingerie, hired a male stripper, lived off caviar for two weeks. What do you think I did with it?"

"You certainly didn't spend it on clothes for Katie."

That made her mad as hell. Just who did he think he was? "Let's get something straight, Deacon. I've been managing pretty well all these years without you. Katie may not dress like someone out of *Vogue*, but her clothes are nice and clean. I don't want her to think money is the answer to everything. And if you want to know where the check went, here." She grabbed a bankbook and slapped it in his hand. "I started a savings account for her. For when she goes off to college."

"I've already taken care of her education. That money was to buy clothes and do things."

"My daughter doesn't need a fifteen-hundred-dollar-a-month allowance! I can't compete with that."

"*Our* daughter. And I don't expect you to compete. But as her father, I naturally want to see that she has what she needs."

Cody shook the book in his face. "This may be the norm where you come from, Deacon, but it's not the way we do things here. I agreed to let Katie visit you, but I never agreed to let you undo all the good things I've taught her." She paused and lowered her voice. "Besides, you don't want Katie loving you for what you can buy her. Let her love you for who you are. Her father."

"You're a fine one to be tossing morals in my face, Cody. After what you've done."

"Deacon Brody, I'm about to ask you to leave before I throw you out of my house!" At his look of surprise, she went on. "I am sick to death of you telling me how I ruined your life, do you hear me!" When he didn't answer, she went on. "I thought I was doing you a favor at the time, you got that? Don't you think I knew how badly you hated being poor? Well, I did. And I wasn't going to take a chance on your hating me because you had to give up your dreams and work in a textile plant." Her voice broke. "Look at you now, Deacon. You have it all. Money. Power. Everything you could possibly want."

It was the first time he had considered the possibility that Cody might have suffered all those years the same as he had, that maybe she had made sacrifices for him. All this time he'd felt duped, rejected, foolish for loving her for so long. Now he realized she had loved him as well. Loved him enough to set him free. Something stirred deep in his heart. She had deceived him, but she had done it out of love. She had wanted him to realize his dreams, with or without her. The knowledge that she would do that for him jolted him to the soles of his feet. He had never known such unselfish caring. But then, he'd never known anyone like Cody. Suddenly, he was embarrassed.

"None of those things meant anything without you," he said.

Cody felt the tears fall. "Deacon, I'm sorry if I hurt you, and I'm even sorrier for betraying you where Katie is concerned. I honestly thought I was doing the right thing. I loved you so much. I didn't want anything to stand in the way of your happiness." She swallowed. "Not even me. Not even . . . our daughter. I know it's too late for us, but it's not too late for Katie. You and Katie have the rest of your lives."

He had not cried since the day they'd buried his sister, but he recognized the signs. His heart ached, his eyes burned. His voice shook when he spoke. "So do we, Cody." At least he hoped as much. Of course there was the chance that he had screwed up again.

At first Cody thought she had misunderstood him. She snapped her eyes up and found him gazing down at her. "What did you say?"

"It's not too late for us. I want to start over."

She took a step back. Already, she was shaking her head. "I can't, Deacon. We're too different now."

"We're the same people we've always been." He smiled gently. "Only I won't have to sneak you into the drive-in movies anymore."

"That's not what I meant. I don't want a mansion in Memphis. I don't want to spend three fourths of my time alone while you tour the country. I don't want to share you with every groupie you meet along the way."

"I won't be touring anymore, Cody."

"What?"

"You heard me. I've had it with that end of the business."

"But, what about your career?"

"I'll perform special engagements now and then," he said, "just to keep the bills paid and my name out there." He smiled. "But what I really want to do is write songs from now on. That was always my favorite part anyway."

Cody was stunned. "So where does that leave us?"

Deacon stepped closer. "I want you, Cody. I want you to be my wife. Only this time I'm not going to let you back out."

She felt as though her knees were about to buckle beneath her. "You mean you still want to marry me? After all that's happened?"

Deacon placed his hands on her shoulders and looked deeply into her eyes. "Cody, I have never once stopped loving you. I may have hated you at times," he added with a smile, "but I always loved you." His look grew so tender, she thought her heart would burst from her chest. "When I think how you sacrificed for me." He paused and shook his head. "Nobody had ever done that sort of thing for me, Cody. Only you. And only you can fill this empty place in my heart. Until I saw you again, I felt as though I'd been in a deep sleep. Life held no true meaning for me. Then I found you, and it was like coming out of a daze or something. Like seeing the sun after months and months of rain. Like spring after the first thaw. Like waking up to a bright summer morning." He squeezed her shoulders. "We can't go back in time and change all that's happened, but we can start fresh. You, me, and Katie. We can be a family."

"But where would we live?"

"I don't give a damn where we live. You want to stay here, fine. We can convert the place back into a house so there'll be room for the babies. Just say you'll marry me, Cody, and the rest will fall into place."

She gazed up at him for a long, breathless

moment. "Oh, Deacon—" She paused and stepped closer and suddenly she was in his arms, where she had always wanted to be. "Of course I'll marry you."

He kissed her then, capturing her lips, pulling her body tightly against his. "You feel so good," he said, muttering the words against her lips. "I want you as much as I did when we were eighteen. Don't ever run from me again, Cody."

"Never," she promised. "For as long as I live, I'll be here for you."

THE EDITOR'S CORNER

If there were a theme for next month's LOVESWEPTs, it might be "Pennies from Heaven," because in all six books something unexpected and wonderful seems to drop from above right into the lives of our heroes and heroines.

First, in **MELTDOWN**, LOVESWEPT #558, by new author Ruth Owen, a project that could mean a promotion at work falls into Chris Sheffield's lap. He'll work with Melanie Rollins on fine-tuning her superintelligent computer, Einstein, and together they'll reap the rewards. It's supposed to be strictly business between the handsome rogue and the brainy inventor, but then white-hot desire strikes like lightning. Don't miss this heartwarming story—and the humorous jive-talking, TV-shopping computer—from one of our New Faces of '92.

Troubles and thrills crash in on the heroine's vacation in Linda Cajio's **THE RELUCTANT PRINCE**, LOVESWEPT #559. A coup breaks out in the tiny country Emily Cooper is visiting, then she's kidnapped by a prince! Alex Kiros, who looks like any woman's dream of Prince Charming, has to get out of the country, and the only way is with Emily posing as his wife—a masquerade that has passionate results. Treat yourself to this wildly exciting, very touching romance from Linda.

Lynne Marie Bryant returns to LOVESWEPT with **SINGULAR ATTRACTION,** #560. And it's definitely singular how dashing fly-boy Devlin King swoops down from the skies, barely missing Kristi Bjornson's plane as he lands on an Alaskan lake. Worse, Kristi learns that Dev's family owns King Oil, the company she opposes in her work to save tundra swans. Rest assured, though, that Dev finds a way to mend their differences and claim her heart. This is pure romance set amid the wilderness beauty of the North. Welcome back, Lynne!

In **THE LAST WHITE KNIGHT** by Tami Hoag, LOVE-SWEPT #561, controversy descends on Horizon House, a halfway home for troubled girls. And like a golden-haired Sir Galahad, Senator Erik Gunther charges to the rescue, defending counselor Lynn Shaw's cause with compassion. Erik is the soul mate she's been looking for, but wouldn't a woman with her past tarnish his shining armor? Sexy and sensitive, **THE LAST WHITE KNIGHT** is one more superb love story from Tami.

The title of Glenna McReynolds's new LOVESWEPT, **A PIECE OF HEAVEN,** #562, gives you a clue as to how it fits into our theme. Tired of the rodeo circuit, Travis Cayou returns to the family ranch and thinks a piece of heaven must have fallen to earth when he sees the gorgeous new manager. Callie Michaels is exactly the kind of woman the six-feet-plus cowboy wants, but she's as skittish as a filly. Still, Travis knows just how to woo his shy love. . . . Glenna never fails to delight, and this vibrantly told story shows why.

Last, but never the least, is Doris Parmett with **FIERY ANGEL,** LOVESWEPT #563. When parachutist Roxy Harris tumbles out of the sky and into Dennis Jorden's arms, he knows that Fate has sent the lady just for him. But Roxy insists she has no time to tangle with temptation. Getting her to trade a lifetime of caution for reckless abandon in Dennis's arms means being persistent . . . and charming her socks off. **FIERY ANGEL** showcases Doris's delicious sense of humor and magic touch with the heart.

On sale this month from FANFARE are three fabulous novels and one exciting collection of short stories. Once again, *New York Times* bestselling author Amanda Quick returns to Regency England with **RAVISHED.** Sweeping from a cozy seaside village to the glittering ballrooms of fashionable London, this enthralling tale of a thoroughly mismatched couple poised to discover the rapture of love is Amanda Quick at her finest.

Three beloved romance authors combine their talents in **SOUTHERN NIGHTS,** an anthology of three original novellas that present the many faces of unexpected love. Here are *Summer Lightning* by Sandra Chastain, *Summer Heat* by Helen Mittermeyer, and *Summer Stranger* by Patricia Potter—stories that will make you shiver with the timeless passion of **SOUTHERN NIGHTS.**

In **THE PRINCESS** by Celia Brayfield, there is talk of what will be the wedding of the twentieth century. The groom is His Royal Highness, Prince Richard, wayward son of the House of Windsor. But who will be his bride? From Buckingham Palace to chilly Balmoral, **THE PRINCESS** is a fascinating look into the inner workings of British nobility.

The bestselling author of three highly praised novels, Ann Hood has fashioned an absorbing contemporary tale with **SOMETHING BLUE.** Rich in humor and wisdom, it tells the unforgettable story of three women navigating through the perils of romance, work, and friendship.

Also from Helen Mittermeyer is **THE PRINCESS OF THE VEIL,** on sale this month in the Doubleday hardcover edition. With this breathtakingly romantic tale of a Viking princess and a notorious Scottish chief, Helen makes an outstanding debut in historical romance.

Happy reading!

With warmest wishes,

Nita Taublib
Associate Publisher
LOVESWEPT and FANFARE

FANFARE

Rosanne Bittner

_____ 28599-8 EMBERS OF THE HEART . $4.50/5.50 in Canada
_____ 29033-9 IN THE SHADOW OF THE MOUNTAINS
$5.50/6.99 in Canada
_____ 28319-7 MONTANA WOMAN .... $4.50/5.50 in Canada
_____ 29014-2 SONG OF THE WOLF .... $4.99/5.99 in Canada

Deborah Smith

_____ 28759-1 THE BELOVED WOMAN .. $4.50/ 5.50 in Canada
_____ 29092-4 FOLLOW THE SUN .... $4.99/ 5.99 in Canada
_____ 29107-6 MIRACLE .... $4.50/ 5.50 in Canada

Tami Hoag

_____ 29053-3 MAGIC .... $3.99/4.99 in Canada

Dianne Edouard and Sandra Ware

_____ 28929-2 MORTAL SINS .... $4.99/5.99 in Canada

Kay Hooper

_____ 29256-0 THE MATCHMAKER, ... $4.50/5.50 in Canada
_____ 28953-5 STAR-CROSSED LOVERS .. $4.50/5.50 in Canada

Virginia Lynn

_____ 29257-9 CUTTER'S WOMAN, ... $4.50/4.50 in Canada
_____ 28622-6 RIVER'S DREAM, ... $3.95/4.95 in Canada

Patricia Potter

_____ 29071-1 LAWLESS .... $4.99/ 5.99 in Canada
_____ 29069-X RAINBOW .... $4.99/ 5.99 in Canada